Four Questions

A Novella

E. Scott Martin

ISBN-10: 1725722798
ISBN-13: 9781725722798

Cover illustration by E. Scott Martin

"O God! Can I not grasp
Them with a tighter clasp?
O God! can I not save
One *from the pitiless wave?*
Is all *that we see or seem*
A dream within a dream?"

Edgar Allan Poe, *A Dream Within A Dream*

CHAPTER 1

The young boy stood with two other classmates in front of a microphone on the school's wooden stage.

For the smiling, beaming grownups in attendance – parents, grandparents, aunts, uncles, teachers – an elementary school spelling bee would not appear to be cause for extreme nervousness.

For the shy, blonde-haired third-grader, however, it was cause for panic, as he tried with great difficulty to keep his legs from shaking.

“Support. S U P P O R T, Support,” said one of his competitors.

“Correct,” said one of the bee's judges. “The next word is 'bravely.'”

"Bravely. B R A V E L Y. Bravely," said the boy's second remaining classmate.

"Correct. The next word is 'amazing.'"

He stepped forward and began to spell the word. "Amazing. A M A Z I N G. Amazing."

The three students thus far had outlasted 120 of their classmates. Many of the competitors, bored with the event, had purposely misspelled their word to get themselves offstage. The boy knew it, and secretly wondered if he should have incorporated the same strategy.

"The next word is 'happening.'"

"Happening. H A P P I N I N G. Happening."

"I'm sorry, that is incorrect." The loser, dejected, stomped off the stage, likely perturbed at having wasted so much time when he could have been elsewhere. There were now only two left.

"The next word is 'plague.'"

The girl of the remaining pair stepped forward to the microphone. She was smart, cocky even. Quite self assured. "Plague. P L A G U E. Plague."

"Correct. The next word is 'picked.'"

Once again, the boy forced himself to the mic. Shuddering, he croaked out "Picked. P I C K E D. Picked."

“Correct.” As much as the blonde-haired boy was nervous, he could detect a frustration in the crowd, too, as he scanned their faces. He saw some yawns, some wristwatches being examined, a few arm stretches. The bee was heading toward the two-hour mark.

“The next word is 'marvel.'”

“Marble,” said the little girl with brown hair, confidently, a full head taller than the boy. “M A R B L E. Marble.'”

“I'm sorry, that's incorrect.” The audience exhaled a part sigh, a part gasp. Though stunned by her error, the girl remained on stage, assured of second place.

“If you can spell 'marvel' correctly, you will win the bee,” said the judge to the boy. The judge made sure to enunciate the word for clarity.

The boy swallowed his scant saliva hard, audibly. Again, he stepped up to the mic, knees shaking, stomach turning. He felt sweaty, hot. His hands were cold.

“Marvel. M A R V E L. Marvel.”

Before the judges could officially proclaim him the winner, the crowd stood and began to applaud. He saw his parents in the throng, hands clapping, proud smiles.

The three judges stood and made their way to the stage to bequeath the awards to the winner and runner up. A trophy and ribbon for each, a check for $50 to the winner, $20 for second place.

The boy, seeing their approach, feeling overwhelmingly queasy, departed rapidly, stage left, his tennis shoes thumping on the wood of the old stage floor. The crowd quickly became quiet in bewilderment.

They found him 15 minutes later, crouched in a stall in the boy's bathroom, his face wet with tears.

At that exact time, 600 miles to the east, two teenage girls in a residential neighborhood leaned against a powder blue Ford Thunderbird in front of a home long abandoned.

“What's the matter?” one asked the other.

“Nothing.”

“You think it's haunted or something?”

“No, you moron.”

“Then what's the deal?”

“We're waiting for Ernie. He said he'd be here.”

The two friends loitered in front of the old Robbins house, empty of permanent human occupants for years now. The platinum blonde goaded her friend with light brown hair.

“It's not like we can't go in right now.”

“So we can smoke cigarettes in there? We can do that out here. And hand me one.”

Platinum-blonde teen handed her friend a smoke, who lit it and began puffing on it nervously.

“He was supposed to be here a half hour ago. That's what he said, right?”

“Yeah. It's what his note said,” said the light-brown haired girl, withdrawing a crumpled piece of notebook paper from her pocket, which simply said “ROBBINS HOUSE 6 PM FRIDAY? LOVE ERNIE.” The scrawl was childish, but legible enough.

“How do we know he's coming? And is he going to bring the stuff?”

“He will. Just shut up and relax.”

“Screw this. I'm outta here girlie,” said the platinum-haired one. “I'm going to Tony's. He'll cover us. You coming?”

The girl with the light brown hair puffed on her smoke and thought for a moment. “No, go ahead. I'll wait here. If he doesn't show up, I'll meet up with you later.”

"OK, later. And tell your dad thanks for the tires."

She nodded her head.

With that, her friend got in the driver's seat, started the car, and turned on the radio. The friend left behind heard the radio's song playing loudly then fading away as the vehicle disappeared down the street.

The girl left behind glanced at her watch. It was only 6:35 p.m. Not yet that dark. She walked to the rear of the old house. Standing on the street without a reason in this small-town residential neighborhood was asking for trouble, usually. Last thing she needed was a trip home in a cop car. Maybe Ernie would show, eventually.

The back door of the home hung loosely on rusty hinges, swinging gently as she stepped inside. The girl with the light brown hair walked deliberately, avoiding leftover debris from past parties. Candle wax, empty beer cans and ashes stained the floors. Spray painted graffiti tarnished the walls.

She walked up the steps, which, though creaky, were still remarkably sturdy for being exposed to the elements and disuse. What used to be the second bedroom on the right is where she and her friends typically partied. Tattered curtains remained to partially block the view from those outside the house.

Entering the room, she saw the curtains had been pulled back. She quickly pulled them shut again.

The room was shabby, but not nearly as abused as the lower floors. Most of the glass still remained in the windows. An empty milk crate sat in the middle of the floor, surrounded by a few empty beer bottles and cans. The room was musty, combined with the lingering aroma of old beer and pot fumes.

She detected a sound, to her left, from the room's closet. Turning, she felt one hand cover her mouth and another grab her arm.

CHAPTER 2

He awoke, breathless, sheets adhering to the sweat of his body.

Though his eyes were open, he was not fully cognizant of his surroundings, a limbo of sorts between the dream world and reality.

His dream remained vivid. It wasn't horrifying, however, and after recovering his bearings, he wondered why he had awakened in this manner.

Turning toward his alarm clock he saw it read 5:26 a.m. – morning, but still dark, and earlier than he planned to arise.

“Damn,” he muttered to himself, as he sat upright, swinging his legs over the side of the bed, connecting his feet to the floor.

The light hurt his eyes as he entered the bathroom. Adjusting himself to the contrast, Heath Hawkins filled a cup with water and took a few gulps. The water from the sink, tepid, metallic, was nonetheless refreshing. Sweat still dripped from his forehead and neck.

Typically, within a few moments after awakening, he would not have recalled details of a dream, pleasant or frightening. This one... this one was different. He remembered everything. Going back to sleep was an impossibility. He prepared for the work day.

Turning on the shower, he stripped off his pajama pants and underwear, and stepped in.

“Late night?”

“Early morning, actually,” Heath replied drowsily, dropping his satchel on his desk and walking past his inquisitive, and way too-perky for 8 o'clock in the morning, co-worker. He made his way to the office break room. A hot cup of coffee beckoned.

Returning to his desk, mug in hand, Heath plopped

into his chair with a sigh and turned on his computer. Same as every day. Same as every day for the past 11 years. His routine was both welcome, as he was not an adventurous type, yet somewhat irritating. Even the non-enterprising may find themselves bored by year after year of the same.

The first hour or so of the day was mostly checking emails and making a few phone calls – a typical start for the courts and crime reporter of the *Brighton Falls Republic*.

“Any good cases today?” asked his perky and inquisitive co-worker, Bridget Parker.

“Nothing too big. Mostly low-level druggies, wife beaters, petty thieves.”

Bridget, a dowdy salt-and-pepper haired woman in her mid-50s with puffy eyelids and no longer possessing natural eyebrows, was always outwardly friendly, but Heath knew she envied his role at the paper. The problem was, when given the opportunity to report on the subjects of “law and order,” she wasn't good at it. The few times she'd been asked to fill in – usually when Heath had a scheduling conflict or during those rare times he took a vacation day – she had trouble utilizing the most basic legal concepts a crime and court reporter should know. Exactly how hard is it to do an internet search and learn the difference between an “arraignment” and a “sentencing?”

Names apparently also posed a problem for Bridget. Misspelling the name of the chairwoman of the Brighton Falls Ladies Fire Auxiliary Pancake Breakfast Committee was forgivable. Misspelling the name of the judge who'd sat on the bench for three decades? Who could possibly misspell “Judge Jones?” She did – twice.

Bridget, who had started at the paper a good 10 years before Heath, and owed her position there by virtue of being the cousin of a former editor, therefore found herself assigned to so-called “fluff” pieces...like pancake breakfasts. She performed this duty with competence, generally.

Even as Heath sent emails, replied to emails, made phone calls, and took notes, the dream stayed with him, floating, as it were, on the periphery of all else.

“Hey Heath, come 'ere.”

He'd heard the request (command, actually) a million times, it seemed. The editor of the *Brighton Falls Republic*, Constance Coleman, was the anti-Bridget Parker. Smart, ambitious. She was about the same age as Bridget, older than Heath, but completely distinct in demeanor and professionalism. Heath appreciated her candor and her commitment to journalism.

She became editor two years after Heath had started with the paper, and had quickly turned things around. She slashed where cuts were needed, and augmented where things needed pumped up. She streamlined and improved the processes by which the publication was put together. Longtime short timers were eliminated while enthusiastic, energetic contributors were hired in their place. She fully embraced the new journalism, giving the digital the same emphasis as ink, if not more.

In short, if Heath envisioned a woman with balls, it was Constance. He was glad she was his boss, because he sure as shit didn't want her job. He also considered her a friend.

For her part, Constance appreciated Heath's product. He wrote concisely and factually – hyperbole be damned. It was why Heath covered grand theft and Bridget covered great grandma's 100th birthday party.

"You get the press release on the prosecutor's race?"

"You bet. Called up Briggs and Potter this morning. Quotes, mugshots. Just need to put it together."

Bart Briggs, Eckworth County's public defender,

had declared his candidacy to run for county prosecutor in the next election. The incumbent, Jake Potter, was retiring and had endorsed Briggs. Unless another candidate unexpectedly jumped in, Briggs was sure to win.

"Good. That'll be our lead for tomorrow. And did you follow up on the Ragsworth lawsuit?"

"Nope. But I will. Unless you want me to hand it off to Trace." Trace Phillips was one of the paper's young reporters, fresh out of college, learning the trade. He also delivered pizza part time, journalism not necessarily being a lucrative field of endeavor.

"Nope. I've got him working on health department reports and dissolutions. And are you kidding? He's not ready for that."

Heath smiled and departed.

Ragsworth Industries was being sued by a group of 20 former employees. The workers had filed a class action civil suit against the company, claiming to have been targeted and fired for reporting unsafe and unfair working conditions at the plant, among other allegations. Ragsworth Industries produced electrical components for industrial machinery around the country and the world. It also happened to be the largest employer in Eckworth County.

The former employees had first sought redress through Occupational Health and Safety Administration. OSHA inspectors reportedly found a few minor violations, but nothing to support the major accusations, including instances where workers had been exposed to hazardous chemicals, forced to work off the clock, and not being given adequate or scheduled break times.

The company was also accused of not reporting or treating properly injuries which occurred during the work day. Out of a job and with virtually nothing to lose, the pink-slipped employees banded together to sue the company for lost wages, damages and medical coverage.

The case would not be heard in Brighton Falls, but in one of Virginia's district courts – if it got that far. The plaintiffs faced an uphill climb.

The lawsuit was the hot topic of discussion over coffee and donuts in Brighton Falls. Its resolution not only affected the fired employees, it loomed over those workers still toiling at Ragsworth Industries, who had been cowed by fear of losing their livelihoods. While they appreciated the efforts of the plaintiffs, and hoped it would lead to an improvement in working conditions, they had mouths to feed, rent to pay, and feet to shoe.

The result also threatened the *Brighton Falls Republic*. Ragsworth Industries, the First Bank of

Brighton Falls, and assorted Ragsworth enterprises, not to mention businesses which made their money from doing business with the Ragsworths – all were advertisers, which is the lifeblood of a print publication. If Valerie Ragsworth, the owner, decided to pull advertising, the *Republic* might not survive. It's both an obvious and a dirty little secret that a publication must walk a fine line between reporting the truth and appeasing the true masters of its purse strings, its advertisers.

The wheels of justice, however, move at a snail's pace. It might be years before the case was finished. Until then, the paper would run the ads and report the news.

"The Ragsworths are rich," Constance had warned Heath once. "And if their money is threatened, they're mean. Really mean. Nasty, even. Do your job, but watch your ass."

The patriarch, Richard "Fox" Ragsworth, had suffered a series of strokes some years back. The once-handsome and powerful local magnate now lay in the private suite of a 24-hour care facility, largely unable to communicate or move. His silver haired good looks a memory.

His wife, Valerie, had taken control of the various Ragsworth concerns following Fox's illness. If anything, the Ragsworth family became even more wealthy when she stepped up and assumed the mantle. If Constance Coleman had balls, Valerie Ragsworth had elephant balls. The cold, calculating thin-lipped matriarch WAS the Ragsworth empire.

Ernie Ragsworth, former high school basketball and football hero, the Ragsworth's only son, occupied an office at Ragsworth Industries, where, rumor had it, the now-balding, fat slob spent the day cruising internet porn, snorting coke and ogling young lady office staffers.

Heath had gathered quotes from the workers and their legal representatives. Good stuff. Heart rending, even. If all he got was carefully crafted statements from the Ragsworth's attorneys, he'd have to roll with it, but Heath really thought the public ought to hear from the witch herself.

As chance would have it, Heath encountered Valerie leaving the bank that very day. Her bank. First Bank of Brighton Falls. Valerie Ragsworth, Director of the Board and majority shareholder.

"Ms. Ragsworth?"

"Yes?"

"Heath Hawkins, reporter with the *Republic*. How do you do?"

Slender, impeccably dressed, she looked at him with a mixture of surprise and irritation. “And what do you want?”

“Thought I'd introduce myself. Don't believe we've met.”

“No, I don't recall meeting you.”

“I'd like to ask a couple questions.”

“I'm rather busy at the moment,” she replied, and turned to walk away, her heels scraping the pavement.

“It's about the lawsuit,” Heath kept pace with her.

“You can speak with my attorney.”

“I've spoken with your attorney. He's not been helpful.”

“Pity.”

“Pity? Really? Is that all you have to say?”

“Yes.”

“I think the public would like to hear your side of the story.”

“They will hear our side of the story in court. Have a nice day, Mr....?”

“Hawkins.”

“Goodbye Mr. Hawkins.”

Returning to the office empty-quoted, Heath's thoughts again turned to the dream. Before going to bed that night, he'd been sitting in front of the TV, watching the news, then some historical documentary about the Lincoln Assassination. He hadn't eaten anything out of the ordinary. And the dream held no monsters, no tornadoes, no childhood trauma, no death or dismemberment. But it was vivid. Every detail, every word, he remembered, clearly.

In his dream, Heath had opened a door and had been blinded by a white light, brighter than the sun. So luminescent, it offended his eyes, and he sought to cover his face with his hands.

Recovering, he began to see details. In the room was a man, about his height, older. The man himself glowed like the room. A full head of white hair, white pants, white shirt. A hairless, tanned face peered over a table full of papers. He shuffled the papers, viewing them with great intensity, seemingly unaware of interloper's presence.

But he was aware. Before Heath could say anything, the man turned to him without surprise and spoke.

“Gracie, North Carolina,” he said. “You'll find there what you seek.”

“What is it I seek?” Heath asked.

"*Narrative of the Santa Fe Expedition*, Volume II, by George Wilkins Kendall."

"I don't understand."

"Within its pages you will find what you seek."

"I... please, I don't understand."

"Go to Orchard Books on Sparrow Street."

Heath was exceedingly frustrated. The man in white displayed no concern.

"Open the pages of the book to find the pages of the book."

"What does that mean?"

"When you return, you may ask more questions. For now, find the book."

Before Heath could interject, he was physically pulled out of the room. The door he had entered slammed shut behind him with a deafening "boom!" It was at that point he had awakened, upset, sweating.

"Open the pages of the book to find the pages of the book," Heath muttered to himself, in recollection.

"What's that?" Bridget asked.

"Nothing. I've got to get to court. See ya." With that, he grabbed his camera and notebook and exited.

Arriving at the courthouse, Heath tried to temporarily push the dream out of his brain. Duty called.

"Hey you, Mr. Reporter Man," called out a voice from behind him as he passed the county auditor's door. He recognized the voice immediately.

"Ricky Dean, always sneaking up on me."

"With this belly? I couldn't sneak up on a dead possum." Ricky Dean let out a boisterous laugh.

Ricky Dean Flynn was the lead detective for the Eckworth County, Virginia, Sheriff's Office. His tall thin legs posed a stark contrast with his large belly, portions of which peeked through his taut dress shirt and fat tie. A belt with gun holster, cuffs and badge hung lazily below his stomach.

Ricky Dean – never Ricky, never Dean – was Heath's best friend, and not coincidentally, his best source of information on criminal happenings. A good 20 years older than Heath, Detective Flynn had taken the reporter under his wing upon his first day with the *Republic*.

"You here for Scotch?"

"Yep, among others," Heath replied. "What's this make, three times this year alone?"

Ricky Dean let out another laugh, paired with a snort. "Sounds about right. Ol' Scotch might as well just have his mail forwarded here to the courthouse... or the jail."

Scotch, in this case, was not an alcoholic beverage, but a certain Charles "Scotch" Hampton, a 78-year-old career petty criminal and semi-celebrity in the community. His frequent presence at the courthouse and the county jail was no exaggeration. Scotch had a lengthy rap sheet, originating in his early teens. Virtually all of his arrests – primarily theft, disorderly conduct, receiving stolen goods, vandalism, public urination – were alcohol related. Even sober, he wasn't "all there" but he had a magnetic personality, was quick with a laugh and not too proud to engage in self-deprecating humor. He knew everyone in Brighton Falls and everyone in Brighton Falls knew him.

His criminal record had yet to completely overshadow his heroism in the Vietnam War, where a young Private First Class Charles Hampton, U.S. Army, had been decorated with a Distinguished Service Cross for driving a tank into an enemy position and killing 12 Viet Cong guerrillas, saving many American lives as they were pinned down in an ambush. Or perhaps it was 13 guerrillas – the Army was never sure on the exact number of enemy dead given the condition of their remains. The fact that he'd been drunk at the time was also quietly overlooked at the awards ceremony.

Ironically, Scotch never drank his nickname beverage. Hated the stuff. Beer, vodka or homemade moonshine were his preferred agents of inebriation. Especially moonshine.

Scotch lived in a cabin in the woods outside Brighton Falls. His living was made handcrafting rough-hewn wood furniture and selling it at the local flea market. Good stuff, and eagerly purchased by locals and tourists. When he wasn't drunk, he lived a modest, yet productive, life.

“Speak of the devil hisself,” said Ricky Dean, as Scotch was led past the two by a sheriff's deputy. The handcuffs on his wrists was a formality.

“Hey Scotch, hanging in there?” asked Heath.

“Hell yes, gonna take more than THE Eckworth County Sheriff to bring this old boy down,” Scotch responded, laughing. The deputy led him into the courtroom to face Judge John Paul Jones.

Jones, purposely named after the Revolutionary War naval hero, was a local, born and raised in the area. As with Scotch, everyone knew him, and he knew everyone. He was stern, but fair, always seeking to make the punishment fit the crime, in the attempt to forestall future criminality and extend mercy when benevolence was warranted.

Heaven forbid, however, a defendant were to display an attitude falling short of respect in his courtroom. Many a sneering young miscreant soon found himself shrinking at the defense table enduring a diatribe straight from the Old Testament if showing the least bit of hubris or arrogance in the wise judge's presence.

“It is no coincidence the Bible has a book called 'Judges,'” Jones had once said.

His attention this day turned to Scotch – the man, not the drink.

“Mr. Hampton, the prosecutor has charged you with one count of theft, a felony of the fifth degree. Do you understand what this means?” inquired Jones.

“Yes your honor, I most certainly do.”

“And has your attorney explained the process of this hearing to you in a way you understand?”

“Yes sir, yes your honor.” Heath, sitting nearby observing the proceedings, saw that Scotch's public defender, Bart Briggs, looked like he was ready to take a nap. In his defense, the barrister had represented the war vet in court an uncountable number of times. He was likely bored.

“The purpose of this hearing is to submit a plea to the court and then be sentenced. After hearing the charge against you, and understanding the facts of the incident, how do you plead?"

"Guilty your honor. Guilty as hell." The court stenographer let loose a barely discernible giggle.

"That'll do Mr. Hampton." Heath almost detected a smile escape the judge's otherwise stony face.

Jones sentenced him to time already served – 6 days in jail – restitution to the victim ($1,200 for the riding lawnmower he "borrowed" and inexplicably placed in a handicapped parking space at the public library, engine removed and nowhere to be found), court costs, and continued probation. The jail only had so much space, needed more for dangerous offenders than an old timer with drunk, sticky fingers.

Once off the record, the judge said, "Scotch, I don't want to see you in here again anytime soon. Understood?"

"You got it your honor. I've learned my lesson." With that, Scotch bowed ostentatiously in the direction of the bench. Jones sighed. "Bailiff, please bring in our next case."

The deputy removed his cuffs and led him out of the courtroom. Scotch winked at Heath as he left. Heath couldn't help but grin and nod as another perp was led into the room to face justice.

CHAPTER 3

It was approximately a two-hour drive to Gracie, North Carolina, from Heath's corner of southwest Virginia. Being the diligent reporter, he had searched online to confirm the details the white-haired man in his dream had told him. To that point, the mysterious oracle had not been lying.

There was a Gracie, North Carolina, population 600. There was a Sparrow Street. And on that street there was an Orchard Books.

Heath decided to use one of his vacation days to travel there. Constance didn't mind. He had plenty of vacation to use, and his news beat had been relatively slow that week. In fact, she'd encouraged him to take some time off, if only a day. He also didn't want to feel rushed.

Besides, the book store was only open on afternoons during the week – a part time venture for its owner.

The early February sky was cloudy and the occasional sprinkle spattered against his windshield. Other than being somewhat hillier and possessing more foliage than his native Indiana, Heath thought there really wasn't much to distinguish these parts with those back home. The Virginia/North Carolina accents, of course, were distinct, but as he'd lived there for more than a decade, he discovered his speech had begun to conform to that of his fellow inhabitants. In other words, he spoke their language and no longer felt so much the carpetbagger in their midst.

And it wasn't as if he had much else he could be doing on his day off. Heath had never married, no offspring. His social life consisted primarily of the occasional night out with acquaintances or when Ricky Dean's wife had him over for dinner with the family. Over the years he had dated, albeit unsuccessfully. No serious relationships had ever developed. There was only one woman he truly loved, which was a long time ago. And he hardly knew her.

Heath pulled into Gracie around noon. It had taken less time than he expected and the bookstore wouldn't open until 1. The town, if it could be called that, had few open businesses along the main street. The remnants of a once-lively village now consisted mostly of empty storefronts, their signs cracked and fading. The window of a abandoned grocery advertised a pack of Marlboros for $1.99 – cigarette pricing from 1985, maybe, he thought. As he drove through the town – old, listless – Heath wondered if "Population 600" was an intentional exaggeration on the part of the village fathers or just negligence.

With some time to kill and a little hungry, he decided to sample the food offered by "Obie's Eats," seemingly the town's sole hot spot.

An hour later, his belly full of surprisingly good country fried chicken, mashed potatoes, gravy, buttered rolls, and peach cobbler, Heath ventured out to find Orchard Books.

This was no big box literary juncture replete with attractive professionals sipping lattes and browsing the "Organic Gardening" section. Orchard Books was a one-story house, with peeling white paint and concrete crumbles of what was once a sidewalk out front. Truthfully, he expected no better.

Parking his car, he noticed the sign in the window said "CLOSED."

"Dammit." He hoped the owner had not passed

away since he'd called her three days before. She sounded as old as the town she lived in. Briefly, he pondered the ridiculousness of driving here, purely on the basis of a dream.

He exited the vehicle and walked to the front door. Peering inside, he saw there were lights on. He grabbed the door's knob and it turned.

"Oh sorry honey," the owner said. Heath observed the aged, heavyset black woman stand up from her seat in front of a small TV. "I forgot to switch the sign."

"Hi. Glad you're open. Are you Ms. Orchard?" asked Heath, quickly masking his short-lived disappointment.

"Yes, that's me. Is there anything I can help you with?"

"No, I was just passing through town here and thought I'd browse." Heath decided long before he would not specifically ask to see Orchard Books' copy of *Narrative of the Santa Fe Expedition*, Volume II, by George Wilkins Kendall. Explanations, he felt, can be tricky things.

"Well, help yourself. If you need me, I'll be right here," she said with a smile, returning to her daytime soap opera and sipping cola from a straw, the sign still telling potential customers the shop was "CLOSED."

He soon found there was little "walking" in the shop. It was more a matter of "side stepping." In addition to books haphazardly placed on shelves, there were stacks upon stacks of books lining the bookshelves, up to his knees, leaving about one foot of space to stand. Heavily read cheap, paperback romance novels with bent spines shared space with hardback copies of *American Heritage*. Fashion magazines were forcibly quartered with high school textbooks from the 1940s. The shop's owner had long ago abandoned any relationship with Melvil Dewey, not to mention the Library of Congress.

Where to begin? How to begin? He had a title, but little else. Searching through thousands upon thousands of disorganized books over the next four hours seeking an obscure book for an indeterminate reason prompted by a dream is not the stuff of a sane mind, he mused. Yet here he was, burning a vacation day, in an old town, in an old bookshop, looking for an old book.

Heath started at the beginning, choosing a shelf toward the front of the shop and tracing the titles with his finger, left to right, top to bottom. He had researched the book some prior to his day trip. It had been published by Harper and Brothers, New York, in 1844. It certainly wouldn't have much in the way of a glossy paper cover, and given its age, was more likely to be found on a shelf than on the floor. That in itself simplified things.

After about an hour, he stopped, briefly. He still disliked the idea of asking the shop's owner for a specific title, especially one so obscure. However, his frustration was growing and his fingers smelled vinegar-like from contact with musty book pages. No, he said, keep looking.

Then, he saw it. Or what he thought was it. On a top shelf, surrounded by similar-looking ancient tomes. The gold leaf writing on its spine had nearly been rubbed away: *Kendall/Santa Fe Expedition/ Vol. I.*

"Ah shit," he exclaimed, seeing it was Volume I and not Volume II.

"You OK back there?" Ms. Orchard asked.

"Sorry, I stubbed my toe. Yes, everything's fine. Thanks."

The shop's proprietor made a "Hmmphh" sound, then returned to her TV show.

Volume I was certainly not Volume II. Nonetheless he flipped through its pages, hoping to be enlightened in some manner. He found nothing extraordinary.

He did, though, have this book. And its appearance would help him find its companion, if Volume II was there.

Hours had passed. Heath even returned to examine previous shelves. Before long, closing time, 4 p.m., approached.

“We're gonna be closing up here soon. You find anything yet?” the owner inquired.

“Yes, but still looking.” Then it struck him. He had the answer in his hands all along.

“Do you have Volume II of this book?”

Ms. Orchard took the volume from him and looked it over.

“This kinda looks familiar,” she said. “Let me think. Let me think.”

With that, she turned around and examined the books on the shelf behind her. He did the same. After a few minutes, however, there was no result.

“I'm sorry honey, I don't think we have the other one to go with this.”

Disappointment clouded his face. “Well, guess I'll have to try some other time.” The shop's clock struck four.

“You come back tomorrow. I'll help you look for it.”

"Thanks, you've been helpful, but I won't be able to come back tomorrow. Maybe another day."

"Sure. Thanks for stopping by."

Heath headed out the door and stepped towards his car. Something made him turn around. One of those things that can't be accounted for by science or math or medicine. As he turned, he saw Ms. Orchard pull up a book from the floor, one she'd used to prop open the interior front door of the shop.

"Hey, wait, hold it!" he yelled.

Heath didn't waste time with further niceties as he pulled out his wallet. He also didn't quibble over the cost of the two volumes – $175. She'd voluntarily cut him a "deal" whereas he could buy each for $100 or both for $175. "There goes more than a couple hours of pay," he told himself. Ms. Orchard grinned broadly. Not a bad day's work watching TV.

As rain lightly sprinkled the windshield of his car, Heath set aside Volume I on the passenger seat, and opened Volume II, which was in much worse condition than its companion.

"Open the pages of the book to find the pages of the book," he whispered, quoting the dream man.

Gingerly, he began turning pages. The edges were quite yellowed, and though the subject matter didn't necessarily appeal to him, he treated the book with caution and a sense of reverence. What was the secret of this book? He still thought himself foolish for having gone to so much trouble because of something likely caused by late night indigestion.

Two-thirds of the way through he noticed something wedged within. "Pages of a book." Different pages. Smaller pages. Two pages, precisely.

CHAPTER 4

The press conference was surprisingly crowded, with reporters from all corners of the United States and some from overseas.

For Heath, it felt unusual to be on the other side of the camera. He'd often joked he had “a face made for print journalism.” Not that his physical appearance was distasteful, but he nonetheless preferred doing the snapping versus being snapped. A natural shyness he'd known since boyhood still lingered.

He thought it enigmatic, as a reporter, how he sought accolades for his work, but otherwise craved an anonymity. His writing, not his face, should be at the forefront, he believed.

"Ladies and Gentlemen," said the university's public relations director. "I'd like to introduce Dr. Howard Ernsby, professor of history and antiquities here at the university, who has headed up the team researching this discovery."

Those assembled then witnessed the learned man deliver a detailed and scholarly, yet discernible, description of the discovery and its authentication.

"While the revelations contained within these pages do not necessarily answer all the outstanding mysteries of the tragedy – and there are many – they do bring us a few steps closer to solving the enigma that is John Wilkes Booth and possibly the role of others in the Lincoln assassination," Dr. Ernsby said.

With that, he motioned for his assistant to remove the covering in order for the press to view the two pages, now encapsulated in protective glass and mounted vertically so that both sides of each page could be viewed. Its uncovering prompted a torrent of camera snapshots from the spectators.

As the press people moved forward to examine the pages, the professor's other assistants handed out papers which transcribed the pages' contents and their historical relevance. Behind the speaker, an overhead projector transmitted a slideshow of the pages, blown up a thousand times their size.

"As you can see, the pages are worn, but in otherwise very good condition," Ernsby said. "Analysis by the university, in cooperation with the National Archives, the FBI, and two other universities, has confirmed their authenticity. The ripped edges of the paper match up perfectly with that extant in the diary."

As exciting and historical as this revelation was, and as vital as his role had been, Heath amused himself by his desire to disappear. Pleased at being an important link in the discovery of the pages, he also possessed a nagging guilt regarding how they had been found. It wasn't truly his doing, and his explanation seemed insincere, at least to him. No one had really questioned his alibi. He was going to play it as just another Civil War buff who, inexplicably, got lucky.

Ernsby continued speaking as the reporters took their photos. "As you can see from the transcript, Booth has written his sentiments to a love interest, in this case almost certainly Lucy Lambert Hale, daughter of Senator John Parker Hale of New Hampshire," he said. "Obviously, these pages were pulled from the book after the fact to avoid embarrassment, and criminal implication, to the senator and his daughter."

"Further, Booth's reference to 'friends in the Government' most certainly creates more speculation for a conspiracy aided by persons in Washington, D.C. – however, unless more evidence comes to light, we may never know the precise identity of the individuals implicated," he added. "And that is all we are left with at this time – speculation."

"As we understand it, an estimated 43 pages are missing from the diary, or more accurately, the date book," Ernsby continued. "It is entirely possible that some pages were written upon and destroyed by Booth himself, were removed by the government after its seizure or by persons unknown after its seizure, or were removed for no reason related to the crime prior to the assassination."

"We believe, based upon our examination, and independently confirmed, that Booth wrote Page 1 before the preexisting diary entries, and Page 2 after. Therefore, unless some other pages emerge, we can go forward with the assumption that Booth's reference to the 'Government's treachery' are his last written words before being shot by Union troops at the Garrett Farm in Virginia."

The overhead projector displayed an easily readable transcript of Booth's words:

Page 1, obverse

My dearest, my beloved Lucy. The light of my life. I know you may never forgive me for this path I have chosen. If all had gone as planned, we would be together forever. I would have come back for you. I will never forget those winter walks with you hand in hand and how earnestly you professed your most secret longings. I pray you someday find a love that surpasses that which we so fondly shared. My name must be hateful and scornful to you now. Know that I loved you even to the last. Take solace in the sincerity of my deed, though you may

Page 1, reverse

draw hatred for our association. What happens to me is of no consequence if it saves our country but your reputation I hope shall remain unsoiled.

The deed is done – et ita factum est – *While I suffer this wretched pain, I yet take satisfaction. Am I fated to be hunted by these damnable people, people who caused such destruction of the country that we once loved – all for the cause of nigger sufferage? The name John Wilkes Booth will be loved or hated. I have always felt it is this poor soul's destiny.*

Page 2, obverse

I fear for this boy with me, who's only crime is to help me to safety. He was not there when I struck vengeance upon Caesar. His hand bears no guilt. Yet if we are taken, he will surely be hanged. Is it not better that he die in the arms of his friend to the fate of a Bardolph? Or that we die bravely facing these soldiers who track us day and night? Our act was not common thievery. I will not suffer a coward's or a thieve's death. And what of our friends in the Government who will surely abandon us? Their sentiment of late had scorned the bearded ape who sat in judgment as a buffoon. Their knives, once so sharp to stab dead

Page 2, reverse

a tyrant, turn upon us. Will God have mercy on them for their own treachery as my bones are laid to rest?

"The FBI analyzed these pages, looking for imprints that may have been transferred to these pages from writing on other pages.," Ernsby continued. "No clear imprints were found, likely due to age or having been pressed tightly within the pages of the book in which these were discovered."

"Speaking of which, I think its time to introduce the man who found these pages – Heath Hawkins. Heath, would you do us the honor," asked the professor, motioning for him to take the podium.

Heath rose from his seat, placed his hands on the edges of the podium and took a deep breath.

"Tell us, how did you find it?" one reporter asked.

"Well, uh, as you can see from the press release, I was at a bookstore, and came across the pages within a book," he responded. In his mind, however, his response was, "Didn't you read the press release?"

"So was this something you had been looking for?" asked another.

"No, I mean, not in particular," Heath said. "I've always been, uh, fascinated I guess by history, the Civil War, things like that. To find something like this is, uh, pretty amazing." The continual infusion of "uhs" made him feel like an idiot attempting to speak with a mouthful of marbles.

"How much do you think the pages are worth? Will you be offering them for sale or put them up for bid?" blurted out another journalist.

"Am I this obnoxious when I'm the one asking questions?" Heath thought to himself. Pausing a brief moment, he answered, "I, uh, that would be hard to say. I mean, they'd be kind of priceless really. Don't you think? And no, I don't plan to sell them."

Dr. Ernsby, sensing Heath's discomfort as the center of attention and wishing to veer the discussion away from the topic of an auction, stepped forward and interjected: "I'd like to make you all aware that Mr. Hawkins here has graciously donated the pages to the university for further study. Once those studies are completed, the pages will be reunited with the Booth diary, under the protection of the National Archives. He has accepted no money whatsoever for the pages. I'd like to personally thank him for his generous donation for the cause of historical research. We owe him a debt of gratitude."

With that, the audience, both in the crowd and on the podium, stood and applauded. Heath's ears turned red and he gave a nervous wave acknowledging their plaudits.

"Thank you ladies and gentlemen," the professor said, concluding the event. "I and members of the team will be available for further interviews at a later date by appointment. Thank you."

After a few weeks, the buzz had largely died off, much to Heath's relief. He'd turned down multiple interview requests. He was content with the knowledge that a priceless historic artifact of American history had been recovered and the circumstances of its discovery were of little consequence. In time, his name would be a footnote, at best. He wanted it that way.

Shunning the spotlight had always been his way. Recognition for achievements welcome, to be sure, but a pesky self doubt and his urge to remain on the sidelines of life invariably popped up its ugly head. From the time he ran off stage during a third-grade spelling bee award to those later days he fretted endlessly over the girl he adored from afar, and then continually failed to act upon his desires until she was out of reach, being the center of attention was his poison.

Dinner at the Flynn house was a welcome diversion. It was no wonder Ricky Dean sported a large belly. His wife Nan was an excellent cook. Her Dutch apple pie was a perennial award winner at the county fair, and no one questioned her ability to coax the most savory flavor from a side of ham. In addition to being foolish, turning down a dinner invitation to sample Nan's culinary masterpieces would be the equivalent of spitting on an empress. Once offered, it was accepted.

Following the feast, Heath and Ricky Dean retired to the front porch of the Flynn estate as the sun set. There was a smoke shared, an after-dinner libation, and a discussion of the matters of the day.

Heath not only liked, but trusted Ricky Dean. Not because he was a cop – as a journalist, he'd seen plenty enough corruption hiding behind a badge. Ricky Dean, though, had an easy going manner about him. Heath considered him "old school." A Norman Rockwell law enforcer in a SWAT team world. Even the perpetrator of the vilest deed would be treated within the confines of the law. Ricky Dean never let his personal feelings interfere with his job, although he had admitted to an internal desire to bust heads, particularly the heads of those who hurt children.

He'd earned his position honestly, working his way up from the academy to beat cop to detective. Perhaps a run for sheriff someday. Detective Flynn was indeed a keen observer, perceptive to things the normal person might not see, or wish to see.

Heath trusted him. And he had to tell someone about his dream. Before it burst away from him beyond his control.

Ricky Dean sat mostly in silence as Heath related the dream, his trip to North Carolina, his discovery of the Booth papers.

“What do you think?”

“I think people who use books as doorstops oughta be arrested and fined.”

Heath groaned. “Seriously.”

The lawman paused, then looked him straight in the eye. “Seriously? The church would probably say you are possessed. A shrink might call you crazy. The stoners would ask what the hell you're taking, and could they have some.”

“Nice.”

Ricky Dean laughed and slapped him on the leg. “Listen, I've seen some weird stuff, unexplainable stuff. Unbelievable shit, even. But if you say that's what happened, I believe ya.”

Now it was Heath's turn to pause. He looked toward the sunset, now almost night, and sighed.

“I wouldn't tell just anyone about it, though,” Ricky Dean said.

“Of course not. But here's what still bugs me. The man in my dream said 'When you return, you may ask more questions.' Now, this could have been a one-shot deal. But it was quite vivid. The most clear-as-day vision I've ever had. Months later the picture, the sensation... it's still there. And who is this anyway? God? An angel? And why me?”

“Good question. I've always felt you reporters and us cops were somewhat alike. We are continually seeking 'the facts.' For different reasons. You – to sell papers. Us – to solve crimes. Ain't that the truth?”

“True.”

“There's one unsolved case that's always bothered me. From years ago. Now, we've never had a lot of crime in this area. Sure, there's drunken fools beating on their drunken wives, or a car being stolen, or the spray paint on the high school. That's typical."

"Go on."

"Have you ever heard of Tilda Pollack?"

Heath thought for a moment. The name sounded familiar.

"I'm not sure."

"She was a young girl who was raped and murdered. Back in 1989. Just a few months after I started with the force here. They found her body in the old Robbins house on Newark Drive. Never did catch the guy who did it."

"No suspects?"

"There were a few. The Sheriff at the time wrote it off as the work of some transient. I wasn't too sure. But I was young, inexperienced. I wasn't one to question things then."

"What made you think it was someone else?"

"Not sure. Intuition maybe? She was a few years behind me in school. And by all accounts she was a wild thing. Some drugs, some sleeping around. Her pop owned the tire shop here in town."

"Pollack Tire and Lube?"

"That's the one. Her old man killed himself a few years later. I was there for that one too." Ricky Dean's voice trailed off. Heath wondered if he should continue to press for details. After a few moments, he was relieved of the decision.

"When she died, she'd been dating Ernie Ragsworth."

"Ragsworth. Ragsworth? As in Ragsworth Industries?"

"Yep. Son of Fox and Valerie Ragsworth. The bigshot Ragsworths. Biggest bigshots in Brighton Falls. Own the bank too."

"A suspect?"

"Briefly. Sheriff brought him in for questioning. The Ragsworths, of course, had the best lawyer money could buy, sitting right there through the whole shebang. And the Sheriff, good man that he was, wasn't no Columbo. Kid walked free the same day. Never booked."

"Do you think he did it?"

"Dunno. He was a spoiled brat, big man on campus then. Drove the best car. The girls flocked to him like flies on a tuna fish sandwich in August. I could see rape, but I didn't see murder in him."

Heath tried to visualize the scene, the people, the girl.

"You still have the files?" he asked.

"Yessireebob. Stop by tomorrow. I'll give you a looksee."

"Deal."

Ricky Dean took a long drag on his smoke.

"Mr. Reporter Man. You want to know if your man with white hair is real? Next time you see him, ask the sumbitch who killed Tilda Pollack."

CHAPTER 5

It was on no particular night of significance that Heath, in his dreams, returned to the white room.

As with the first, this dream voyage was lucid.

“Who are you?” Heath asked the tan man with white hair, who continued to shuffle his mysterious paperwork upon the massive table.

The specter looked at him, stared through him really, and without saying a word in reply, Heath knew he'd get no answer to this query.

“You said I could ask further questions.”

“Yes.”

“That was a question.”

“Do you wish to use your questions for this reason?”

Instantly, Heath knew what question he should ask. And apparently the man knew what he would ask, in fact, expected him to ask.

“Who killed Tilda Pollack?”

The man narrowed his eyes and displayed a small grin. Almost devilish to Heath's observation. It was chilling.

“Pop's Auctions. June 10. Lot #87.”

The answer stuck, permanently tattooed on Heath's brain. The white-haired man then pointed to Heath's right, but as he turned to see what it was the mystery man wished to show him, he was again whisked from the room to awaken sweaty and shaken in his bed.

Heath decided not to say anything about the dream, yet, to Ricky Dean. First, he remained unconvinced it was no more than a hallucination, despite the veracity of the first dream. No need to get his hopes up if it was a one-time event, he thought. Second, the auction was still five days away. Patience was needed.Pop's Auction House occupied a brick building just east of Brighton Falls. Part auction house, part flea market, part gathering place for bargain hunters and bullshitters.

No one living was sure who “Pop” was. The progenitor of the business had long passed and for all anyone knew, Pop's had been around since General Thomas "Stonewall" Jackson had led his troops through Brighton Falls to intercept and whip three Yankee armies in the Shenandoah Valley in 1862.

Heath obtained the auction listing. It contained a hodge-podge of items from various estates. Household utensils, hand and power tools, curios, guns, sports collectibles, record albums, books, fishing gear, furniture, coins – a little something for everyone.

The description for Lot #87 simply said "Miscellaneous." Which further tormented Heath. The white-haired man's answers were maddeningly translucent. Bidders would not be able to view the items until the morning of the auction.

Until that time, he wanted to learn more about the unsolved murder case. True to his word, Ricky Dean had allowed Heath the opportunity to view the Tilda Pollack case files.

All records of the murdered teen were contained in two cardboard file boxes marked "Pollack, Matilda Marie, Case #9377."

Heath viewed the evidence page by page.

Handwritten notes mingled with typed pages and photos.

"Victim last seen wearing blue jean shorts, white short sleeve cutoff top, brown leather sandals, silver hoop earrings, gold ring with peridot stone on her right hand, engraved wristwatch on her left, acc. to mother. Earrings, ring, wristwatch not located."

As he read the reports, his eyes often returned to the photographs of the victim accompanying the files. Among them was her sophomore year photo.

Tilda was a pretty thing, he thought. Slender, petite, light brown hair, blue eyes, some freckles, demure smile. 1989 was the era of "big hair" for the girls, and Tilda didn't disappoint. Heath wondered how long it took her to get that hairdo ready for the day.

Though he was a reporter, and rooting through other people's business was part of the job description, Heath couldn't help but feel a voyeur. He sat at the sheriff's station examining every known detail of this girl's life story, from its beginning to its brutal end. He soon felt like he knew her.

The coroner's report was cold, technical, and gruesome. Tilda had fought her attacker. The authorities, however, had not been able to match the DNA from the blood and skin cells under her fingernails with any known perpetrator. She had been vaginally penetrated, but there had been no recoverable semen sample. Tilda's death had been attributed to having the breath choked from her lungs. Two sets of hand prints around her bruised throat were the telltale sign. Heath felt his stomach turn viewing the photos of the crime scene.

Toxicology results showed traces of marijuana and alcohol in Tilda's bloodstream, but not in excess. She had not been high or drunk the day of the murder. She died sober.

The investigators had determined the murderer was almost certainly male. That was about as far as they got. Killed for her jewelry was the likely motive, investigators concluded. The sexual assault a sickening bonus for the perpetrator.

Heath viewed printouts of fingerprints collected at the scene – at least seven different people. No surprise at a house long abandoned and taken over for drinking and drug use. The Robbins house at 729 Newark Drive was demolished some years later as a nuisance property. It was now an empty lot.

Heath also read the collected interviews with prospective suspects, Ernie Ragsworth included. The report noted Ernie was a suspected user of narcotics. He had an alibi, however – attending a high school athlete's conference a few hours away – and his story was backed by several witnesses, including his parents, coach and teammates. With Tilda's valuables missing, the "transient murderer" theory made sense, on the surface.

The last person to see Tilda alive was Lydia Cribbs, now Lydia Howell. In her witness statement, she recounted how they had driven to the Robbins house, and she had left her there. Presumably under pressure, Lydia had confessed to investigators the reason why she and Tilda had gone there. Underage drinking was frowned upon in 1989, but marijuana usage was a bigger "no-no" then. No charges were pressed, however.

"Didja solve the case, Mr. Reporter Man?" asked Ricky Dean, entering the room, coffee cups in hand.

"No," Heath replied. "But I've got a feeling you may be getting a tip soon."

"Are you Lydia Howell?" Heath asked.

"Yes. And who are you?"

Though Heath had expected to see some years on Lydia, she appeared virtually unrecognizable from her 1989 persona. Far from the chubby faced teen she had been, driving the powder-blue Ford, she was gaunt and haggard. Skeletal, even, Heath thought. Her once-platinum blonde hair was now gray.

Lydia lived on the outskirts of Brighton Falls in a mobile home park. Her trailer was dingy, dark, and surrounded by garbage and clutter. She stood barefoot on the cracked concrete steps leading to the trailer's door with a torn screen. A TV played loudly within the trailer, and Heath detected the sound of children playing, or fighting. A dog barked in the distance.

“I'm Heath Hawkins, from the *Republic*. I'd like to ask you some questions.”

“About?” the woman said, incredulously, as she took a deep drag from her cigarette.

“About Tilda Pollack.”

Lydia exhaled, blowing not a small amount of smoke in Heath's face. He sensed trepidation.

“Nothing much to say, really,” she said. “Long time ago. I told the cops what I knew.”

“Yes, but do you remember anything else? I've looked at the file and read your statement to the police.”

“Nope.”

“Nothing?”

“Nope.”

Heath considered asking her if she even cared about her friend's death, but it was obvious she'd moved on. Still, he persisted.

“What about her boyfriend? Ernie? Do you think he could have done it?”

Lydia hesitated. “No,” she said, taking another puff from her smoke. “I don't think he did it.”

“You were the last one to see her alive. You don't recall anything unusual?”

“Nope. Ernie said he was going to meet us there, but he didn't show. Then I left and she stayed. Last I saw her.”

“He told you he was going to meet you there?”

“Yeah. He left her a note.”

“A note? What did it say?”

“Just said, 'I'll meet you at Robbins House at 6,' or something like that.”

“What happened to this note?”

“Hell if I know. Tilda had it when I left.” Interesting tidbit, Heath thought, recalling there was no note among the evidence collected by investigators.

At this point, the two were interrupted by a car pulling up to the home.

“Who the fuck is this?” bellowed a man exiting the car.

Before Heath could answer, Lydia interjected, “Drake, now y'all shut up. He's a reporter. He came here to ask me some questions.”

This “Drake,” a burly, bald fellow with grease-stained hands and a Fu Manchu mustache, presumably Lydia's “better half,” approached Heath. He was dressed in a Ragsworth Industries work shirt.

“Questions? About what?”

“He was asking me about Tilda. You know, that girl who died years ago?”

“I don't know any Tilda. And neither do you,” Drake said to his thin partner standing in the doorway. He then glared at Heath.

“Drake, dinner's on. Mr. Heath here was just leaving,” she said. Lydia took another drag from her smoke as her partner brushed past her, giving Heath every indication it was time for him to go.

Having struck out with Lydia, Heath decided to write a story on Tilda's unsolved death, partly to reignite interest in the case, and perhaps bring forth more information that would finger her killer. The Ragsworth civil suit was in slow motion mode.

Tilda's mother Frances, or "Franny," had declined to be interviewed at all, however. Heath's knock on her door was met with a kindly, "No thank you, you have yourself a nice day." The door was shut.

Now a recluse mostly, Franny Pollack had sold her late husband's tire business soon after his suicide. The new owners of the shop had kept the same name all these years. Continuity counted in Brighton Falls.

Once Heath's story was published, many townspeople spoke of remembering the day Tilda's body had been found, the speculation on the perpetrator, how maybe she'd "had it coming." No taboo speaking ill of the dead. She was a wild girl, after all.

Even Ernie, Tilda's former boyfriend, provided his two cents, mailing a letter to the editor accusing Heath and the paper of "digging up painful memories from the past" and "exploiting Tilda's murder to sell papers." Both Heath and Constance suspected Ernie was more upset at being mentioned in the article being questioned by investigators as a person of interest than he was distraught over the death of his former girlfriend.

The letter, handwritten, appeared childish to Heath, with sloppy penmanship, numerous misspellings, and generally poor grammar.

"Is he retarded?"

"That's not very politically correct," snorted Constance, who, herself, was not politically correct.

"OK, maybe it's the drugs. Or multiple concussions."

"I wouldn't doubt it."

After some editing to make Ernie's letter readable, Constance printed it. She was fair even when assertions were incorrect.

Unfortunately, no new clues were forthcoming. For the moment, the identity of Tilda's murderer remained a mystery.

Two days before the auction, Heath was covering a business opening its doors in Brighton Falls – a new pizza joint. Ribbon-cutting, chamber of commerce speeches, all that.

Ernie Ragsworth was there, the family's representative for the chamber this day. Other than his broad shoulders on a 6-foot-3 frame, little remained to indicate he'd once been an athlete – obese, bad complexion, hair a thinning shambles. He looked nothing like his father in his prime, nor himself, if he'd had a prime. It was more than mere age, Heath thought. It was as if he'd just given up trying to look presentable. But then, why should he? He had money, a position in society. Who could he possibly seek to impress?

The heir to the Ragsworth fortune looked at Heath, and it took him a moment to match the name to the face.

“Hawkins, right?”

“Yep, that's me.”

“That story you wrote. What the hell?” Ernie moved in close to Heath, many inches closer than normal comfort allows. A tactic of a bully.

“Story?” Heath replied, raising an eyebrow with purposeful ignorance.

“Yeah, the one about Tilda Pollack.”

“Oh, that.”

“That's bullshit man. Why would you bring that up again?” His bloated face became red.

Heath didn't like the direction this conversation was heading.

“I thought perhaps someone would remember something and help solve her case,” he offered.

“She was my girlfriend. I loved her. I never would have hurt her.”

“I understand that.”

“You did that just to sell papers.”

“No, I did that because her story deserved to be told after all these years. And her murder is still unsolved.”

“And my mom... you better quit bothering her too,” said Ernie, switching gears.

“Your mom?” Again, with purposeful ignorance.

“Those people who filed that lawsuit were just lousy workers. Trying to milk us for money. Everybody's always trying to rip us off.”

Heath merely nodded.

“That's what happens when you're rich. People try to rip you off,” Ernie reiterated, making extra sure Heath recognized they were wealthy.

“I suppose that could be the case.”

“This wouldn't even be a thing if you'd quit writing about it.”

Heath realized conducting a logical, genial conversation with the younger Ragsworth was an impossibility.

“It was nice to meet you Ernie. Have a good one.”

Ernie shot him a dirty look. Heath disengaged himself to speak with others.

As Heath lingered after the ceremony, gathering quotes taking snapshots, he felt he was being watched. It was a sensation difficult to pin down, but he could “feel” a set of eyes looking right through him. And it wasn't Ernie.

As crowds of people filed into the building to

sample the new restaurant's wares, he saw a middle-aged woman pushing a wheelchair on the sidewalk nearby. More than a wheelchair, really. It was oversized and on it reclined a woman, age indeterminate, her black hair streaked with white. Underneath a blanket, he could tell her bony body was twisted into an uncomfortable pose. Hands held fingers that no longer fully functioned. Her tongue fell loosely from her agape mouth and sunken cheeks.

Her eyes, however, her eyes were alive and stared at him, following him no matter her position. They were wide open and deep blue.

“Traveler,” she said, loudly and clearly.

“What's that hon?” asked her caregiver.

“Tra...ve...ler.” Her eyes stayed locked on Heath.

The caregiver then noticed him standing there. “Hi. This is Becky. She loves meeting people.”

“Hi Becky. I'm Heath Hawkins. It's nice to meet you.” He took hold of one of Becky's hands and gave her a gentle handshake.

“And sorry, Mr. Hawkins, she sometimes gets fixed on something and starts babbling. It can make people uncomfortable.”

“No problem at all. So who's this traveler you're talking about, Becky?”

“Traveler,” said Becky, who raised her right arm feebly. Heath would've sworn she was trying to point at him if her fingers had been working.

“Dunno. She's got a mind of her own,” said Becky's caregiver. “She'll go days without making a sound, then alluva sudden she says something. Hard to make heads or tails of it.”

“Well, take care Becky, I need to get going,” Heath said. The caregiver smiled. Becky continued to stare in his direction as he walked away.

CHAPTER 6

That same night, Heath had a dream. No white-haired mystery man in this. Instead, a trip to his past.

He was back in high school. Forget the fact his former learning place had been demolished for a new school. Familiar faces were all around – teachers, classmates, even a few faces from that time which had no business being there. The halls were filled with laughter, chatter, bustle.

Heath found himself sitting in a classroom, with a teacher speaking. Within the setting of his dream, he was aware he'd graduated from this place many years ago. Nonetheless, he had returned, in his teenage body but possessing his adult mind. He viewed the classroom, the students, all as real as the day he'd last been there.

"Mr. Hawkins," said a voice. "Mr. Hawkins."

Heath turned his attention to the teacher.

"Mr. Hawkins, what do you think Keats meant when he wrote 'Beauty is truth, truth beauty?'"

Only Mrs. Gill, he thought to himself, still fully aware he was dreaming.

"I think he was saying that some see beauty in truth, while others see truth in beauty." Heath cringed the second he finished his response. It was said quickly and without much thought.

The austere instructor looked at him briefly, then cast her gaze to his classmates. "Is he right?"

No one answered.

"Class, is he right?"

"Is Mr. Hawkins right?"

"Is he right?"

Heath turned, hoping someone, anyone, would support his assertion. Instead, the classroom was empty. He turned back to the teacher. She too was gone.

Perplexed, he rose from his seat and walked to the hallway, which was deserted despite being packed with students only moments before.

He walked from room to room, hall to hall. All empty.

A potent loneliness began to overwhelm him. He sought to exit the building.

Pushing open the double doors, he descended the concrete steps of the school. Looking up he was struck by the presence of a large crowd, all facing him, looking at him in complete silence. Each face was expressionless.

Heath slowly stepped toward the wordless, inscrutable assembly. As he got closer, the group began to back away, creating a path for him.

Then he saw her, the object of his teenage desire. The crowd separated, creating a circular space around the two. She turned and smiled upon seeing him, those brown eyes of hers pulling him in like a magnet. It was her eyes which had first drawn his attention to her all those years ago. They were mesmerizing, a mystical combination of sadness and glee that he found perplexing and irresistible.

Heath's high school crush, with her beautiful dark eyes and flowing brown hair, stood before him, youthful and exuberant, just as he remembered her. All others, still standing, watching silently, ceased to exist to him.

The two embraced, kissed. It was slow and passionate. Something that had never happened in reality. He savored her scent, the softness of her lips, her breathlessness, and his. Still aware he was dreaming, Heath willed himself to stay, praying it would never end.

But it did. Heath's ears were bombarded with angry, vexed shouts. Unseen hands grabbed him, lifting him to face the sky, pulling him away. She remained in place, her head slightly tilted in curiosity as she saw him taken.

The dream resurrected a memory, a real one, of a conversation he had with his uncle when Heath was 16, and of advice he regretted not taking.

“Are you dating someone?” his uncle had asked as the two checked the fluids in Heath's Chevy.

“No. There is this girl I like. A lot.”

“So why haven't you asked her out?”

Teenage Heath pondered the question for a moment, then said, “I don't know. I guess I'm afraid she'll reject me.”

“And what if she does? What difference does that make?”

“It would be devastating.”

“I would consider it liberating more than devastating. If she says 'No' you get a definitive answer. Definitive answers are good. The truth is good. Always. You move on to another.”

"Still..."

"Tell you what. You want to attract this girl? Act like you've been there before."

Heath tilted his head, somewhat perplexed.

"Act like you've been there before, dammit." His uncle was not one to mince words. "Have you ever dated ANY girl?"

"No, I haven't." Heath confessed, embarrassed of being a 16-year-old virgin in the presence of his Vietnam War veteran uncle, whom he expected, with some justification, had probably fathered multiple children from Saigon to Sandusky.

His uncle sighed, though he remained sympathetic to his nephew's plight. "Here's what you do. You walk up to her..."

"What if she's with her friends? She's always with her friends it seems."

"You walk up to her," the older man said, ignoring Heath's protest. "You merely say 'Hi' or 'How's it going?' or whatever it is you guys say these days. That's it."

"That's it?"

"Yes."

"What if she doesn't say 'Hi' back?"

"Then you walk away. In fact, even if she DOES say

'Hi' back, you walk away."

"Hmmm..." Heath found this piece of wisdom most curious.

"Another thing," his uncle added. "Don't walk away immediately. Look her over for a couple seconds. Give her a little nod."

"I think I should be writing this down," said Heath, already a budding reporter at heart.

"Listen...and absorb," Heath's uncle replied, with a hint of exasperation. "You walk up to her, greet her, whether or not her friends are there. If she has a boyfriend, and he's there, that's a bonus."

"Really? A bonus?"

"Of course, 'really.' I'm not saying go plant a kiss on her in front of him, but if you show you have the guts to walk up to her, with her boyfriend present, and say 'Hello,' what does that tell her about you? It tells her two things: First, you're not scared of anyone, her or her boyfriend or her friends. Second, she will see you are interested in her, without you actually SAYING you are interested in her."

"Got it... I think."

"Walk up to her like you've done this before. You look her in the eye and say 'Hi' – just to her, no one else. Give her a brief once over, nod, squint your eyes a little, and give her your smallest of small smiles. Then walk away."

The teen's face expressed doubt.

"Let's see you try it."

"Here?"

"No dummy, talk to the cucumbers in the produce section at IGA. Of course, here! Now walk over there, then walk towards me and pretend I'm this stupid 'group' your girl hangs with or whatever and do your thing."

Heath stood, took a few steps back, walked towards his uncle, and said "Hi."

"Close your mouth when you smile. You look ridiculous. Try it again."

The teen, trying to suppress a giggle, walked away then walked back, this time with much less smile.

His uncle, his grease-covered arms crossed, oil-filter wrench in hand, offered more pointers.

"Squint your eyes a little more. And put your hands in your pockets. You want to look casual, relaxed."

Heath repeated the procedure. "Hi."

"Needs work. Try it in front of a mirror when you get home. What's this girl's name anyways?"

"Anne. Anne Ross."

The day of the auction. Heath went to withdraw some cash from the ATM. He had no idea how much he might need for Lot #87. He then recalled how his first dream had cost him $175.

“Better make it $300,” he said, just to be sure. He didn't want to take any chances, despite how it would put a crimp on his electric and water bills.

The parking lot at Pop's Auction House was already filling rapidly as he arrived. It was a Saturday, and not much else was going on in town on this humid summer day.

Over the years, Heath was amazed at both the faces he knew, and those he didn't, after more than a decade in Brighton Falls. The day's auction attendees were a good mixture of both.

One recognizable face that didn't escape notice was his courthouse “buddy” Scotch. The war hero-petty criminal appeared to be perfectly sober as he conversed loudly with friends before the proceedings started. “Perhaps he's given up the booze after all,” Heath thought. “Good for him.”

During the viewing period, Heath went out of his way to examine a variety of lots. He didn't want to beeline to #87 or appear fixated on it, lest he draw attention to it. He'd also planned to place some bids on other lots, to distract fellow auctiongoers from seeing his true intention for being there.

The lot itself seemed unremarkable. A shoebox-sized box, filled with all manner of small items: tokens, keys, old matchbooks, marbles, bottle openers, keychains, costume jewelry, and postcards, from what he could tell. The items had once been important to someone, somewhere. Again, he didn't linger unnecessarily or shuffle through the box, in an attempt to appear nonchalant. Though the dream-man's instructions remained vivid in his mind, he did harbor a small doubt. What if he'd misheard the lot number? What if the white-haired man was just fooling with him?

The auctioneer, a tall beanpole of a man, his huge hands cradling a microphone, and wearing a cowboy hat, blue jeans and a western-style short sleeve shirt emblazoned with small rhinestones, explained the auction's terms and conditions to the crowd, then started his "Hey now, who'll gimme" chant to kick off the festivities.

Heath waited patiently to place a serious bid on the true item he desired. As the auction progressed, he placed bids on some minor lots, nonetheless pulling out of the bidding quickly before they sold.

The moment of truth arrived.

“Here we have lot #87, miscellaneous items,” bellowed the auctioneer. “What we got in there, Carl?”

“Looks like a little bit of everything. Keys, cards, marbles – a true treasure chest!”

The bidders laughed.

“Hey Carl, let's make this more interesting. Throw in #88. What's in 88?”

The auctioneer's assistant lifted over his head a jewelry box. “Lot #88 is a jewelry box, containing some wound-up necklaces. Bottom drawer's locked, no key.”

“OK, who'll gimme ten dollar, ten dollar, ten dollar...”

Heath raised his card. Carl pointed to him and went “Hee-yup!”

Others placed bids, and Heath matched them. He was damn irritated at the auctioneer forcing him to bid on the jewelry box when all he wanted was the shoebox.

“Thirteeee dollars, who'll gimme thirteeee dollars?”

“Hee-yup!” Carl pointed to Heath.

“I got thirteee, I got thirteee, who'll gimme thirteee five, who'll gimme thirteee five?”

"Hee-yup! We got us a Scotch bid here!" This time, Carl pointed to Scotch. In his fixation on the lot, Heath hadn't realized who his competitor was.

"Forty!" Heath yelled.

"I got fortee, I got fortee, I got fortee... who'll gimme fifteee, who'll gimme fifteee...?"

""Hee-yup!" Again, Carl pointed to Scotch.

Heath was fed up. "Dammit Scotch, I will give you $50 if you quit bidding, and I'm going $60 on the lot!"

"Hee-yup!"

The crowd, including Scotch, laughed. "Sold," he said.

"I got sicksteee, I got sicksteee, I got sicksteee, who'll gimme sickstee five, who'll gimme sickstee five? No sickstee five, no sickstee five, no sickstee five.... Sickstee dollars, SOLD, to the gentleman with the sour look on his face."

Again the bidders laughed. Heath rolled his eyes, but managed a pained grin. He walked over to Scotch and handed him a $50 bill. The old vet grinned.

"I was just gonna fix that jewelry box. Looks like it could be a nice one. Must be some heap big important wampum in there for ya, chief," Scotch said, pocketing the $50.

"Let's hope so."

Upon returning home, Heath examined the objects in the shoebox. He spread them out on his bedspread. Nothing appeared to be the linchpin which would unravel the mystery of Tilda Pollack's untimely death. Of particular interest were the postcards, of which only one had been mailed. A picture of the Statue of Liberty. On the back a quick note from someone named "Virgil" to "Ben," dated 1912, asking how his trip to Baltimore had been. The others appeared to be produced during the same era. Certainly not evidence of a murder in 1989.

His attention turned to the keys and coins, then the costume jewelry. None appeared to be of much value, he thought.

He then looked at the jewelry box. It was made of heavily varnished cedar wood, finely crafted, with three drawers and a flip top lid. Could it be possible, he thought, that Lot #88 was what he was supposed to find? Did his oracle know it would be joined with Lot #87?

With some trepidation, Heath opened the top of the box. He withdrew a number of necklaces – some silver, some of undetermined metallurgy, all hopelessly tangled. He placed them with the other items on the bedspread.

He then opened the top drawer. It was empty. The second drawer contained, for lack of a better term, "junk" – some old keys, a pulltab from a soda can, and corroded pennies.

He then attempted to open the bottom drawer. It was locked, as the auctioneer had stated. None of the keys from either lot fit. Heath went to the kitchen, reached into his junk drawer and withdrew a small flathead screwdriver. Returning, he first tried to jimmy the lock, without success. He then carefully wedged the screwdriver in the space above the drawer, at the same time shaking the box. The drawer broke loose. The items from the drawer fell onto the bedspread.

Scotch had been correct. Contained within was indeed some "heap big important wampum."

CHAPTER 7

"So, do we have a case?"

Ricky Dean, wearing white linen gloves, poked at the silver hoop earrings, the gold ring with peridot stone, and the engraved wristwatch. On its reverse, the watch bore the initials M. M. P. – Matilda Marie Pollack. A crumpled piece of notebook paper contained the crudely written words, "ROBBINS HOUSE 6 PM? LOVE, ERNIE." On the other side of the paper were written the words, seemingly in a different hand, "You are forever mine now. He can't have you."

"Geezus Heath...Geezus," he replied.

"Is it enough?"

Ricky Dean took a deep breath, leaned back in his chair, and put his hands behind his head.

"It's not so much a matter of having a case – there's always a case – it's more about having a conviction."

"OK, do we have a conviction?"

"I'd say it's sketchy."

"Sketchy? We have Tilda's jewelry. We have the auction records on who submitted the jewelry box for sale. We have initials on the jewelry box. We may have fingerprints and DNA on the jewelry box and the jewelry, and maybe the note. We have his handwriting on the note. Though one is crudely scrawled, it's obvious it was written by the same person. Lydia told me about this note. And we have Tilda's mother's positive ID on the jewelry. He was never questioned...."

"And he won't be," interjected the detective. "Ain't gonna happen."

"All we need is a DNA test, prints, and measure his hands to see if they match the hand prints on Tilda's neck. We've got the note, Ricky Dean, we've got the note!"

"Heath, it's more complicated than that. You've watched too many crime shows on TV."

“Dammit Ricky Dean!” This was the first time Ricky Dean had ever seen Heath get this angry. “I don't care if the son of a bitch is dead and in his grave. This girl was murdered. She deserves justice. Her mother deserves justice!”

Ricky Dean looked at him. He sympathized. He truly did. But he knew the reality, and the consequences, of what Heath was asking him to do.

“Here's what I can do,” he told his incensed reporter friend. “I will present the evidence to the prosecutor's office. If he feels there's the possibility of conviction, he will present the case to the grand jury. That's the best I can do.”

“OK, fair enough.”

Ricky Dean sighed. “But let me tell ya something – gonna be one helluva jury in this town that would convict Fox Ragsworth of murder.”

Heath was eating lunch at his desk two days later when Ricky Dean walked into the Republic's office. Along with him was Jake Potter, Eckworth County Prosecutor.

“Hey Heath, got a few minutes?”

“Sure, let's go to the conference room.” Heath put down his sandwich. He looked into his boss's office and motioned for Constance to join them. He'd already filled her in on the discovery of Tilda's jewelry and the note, although not the circumstances that led him to the find.

The four went to the conference room and shut the door.

“It's a no go,” blurted out Ricky Dean.

“What?” Heath replied, incredulously.

“Heath, while we appreciate you finding, and turning in, Ms. Pollack's jewelry, the note, everything, there is just not enough evidence to conclusively tie it to Mr. Ragsworth, or any of the Ragsworths,” said the prosecutor.

“You've got to be freaking kidding me!”

“Heath, Heath,” Constance cautioned. “Hold on, let's hear him out.”

Heath shut his mouth, grudgingly.

“Circumstantially, it would be a good case which we might normally pursue,” said Potter. “Yes, we have the auction records showing the jewelry box was consigned by Ernie Ragsworth, but with the time that's elapsed, the lack of any good, solid eyewitnesses, and the tenuous manner in which the jewelry and the note can be tied to Mr.

Ragsworth – can we prove conclusively he wrote the note or placed the jewelry there? – there's just not enough at this juncture to put together a strong case. It would be a waste of time to present this to the grand jury."

"No, what I'm hearing is, you're leaving office in January, the Ragsworths have the best lawyers money can buy, and you don't want to dick with it. THAT'S what I'm hearing," Heath replied.

Potter fell silent. Ricky Dean pursed his lips in an uncomfortable fashion.

"Jake, are you absolutely certain the grand jury wouldn't see the merits of this case?" Constance asked.

"If I may be candid, as much as the Ragsworths are hated, or loved – or feared – in this community, I see no chance, no chance whatsoever, that the grand jury would indict Fox Ragsworth for rape and murder," Potter said. "The man has been an invalid for years. He can't testify on his own behalf. He could never be brought to appear in the courtroom. A deposition of any sort is impossible. And yes, the Ragsworths do have the best money lawyers can buy, Heath. Their attorneys would make this look like we're trying to hang a man who's already half dead."

Heath remained silent, smoldering.

"Heath, there's so many more cases that need to be tried," Potter continued. "People who are committing real crimes right now, today. The jail has to let people go before their damn sentences are completed. Do you know how aggravating it is to our office to try these punks and then have them walk out after a month? Then see them in court again a week later? And what if Ragsworth was found guilty? What then? Let me tell you what would happen – best case scenario. He would be placed under permanent house arrest and continue to live like a vegetable at that rest home he's already in. In other words, nothing changes."

"But what about a civil suit?" Constance asked. "Could Mrs. Pollack sue the Ragsworths?"

"She could," Potter said. "But again, it would be a long shot. And it would bankrupt Mrs. Pollack. She doesn't have the money, or the guns, to take on Valerie Ragsworth."

Heath looked at Potter. He turned toward Ricky Dean, then Constance.

"Fine. But this isn't going away. This is not going away. Not even close." Heath rose, and left the room, slamming the door behind him.

Nursing a beer at the local dive, Heath was absorbed in his own thoughts. Though he hadn't been present, he'd heard Ricky Dean's description of Franny Pollack breaking down when called in to identify her daughter's jewelry.

It was open and shut, to him at least. The jewelry box had Fox Ragsworth's mother's name – Grace Emilia Foster Ragsworth – inscribed in gold leaf on the bottom. Ernie Ragsworth had consigned the jewelry box to auction, likely to feed his three-decades-long drug habit, though he'd never been arrested or convicted on such activities.

Was it possible Ernie was the one who had raped and murdered Tilda? Not likely, thought Heath. Taking such elaborate effort to hide the murder souvenirs, in all likelihood revisited time and time again to relive the sick moment, then inexplicably putting them up for sale in an auction? It didn't make sense. Besides, Ernie had a rock solid alibi for that evening, attested to by a good number of witnesses, including teammates and coaches. And the "neat" handwriting on the one side of the note looked damn close to examples of Fox's writing that Heath had seen. Ernie's childlike scribbling was different. This note was deliberately made to look like someone else's writing. Valerie Ragsworth? The woman would have trouble bending a drinking straw, much less strangling a teenage girl. No, it had to be Fox. Who else had access to these items? The puzzle was incomplete, but the picture was clear. There was no question in Heath's mind. It was infuriating, but what next?

"Don't drink alone, Scarlett," a familiar voice said. "People find out and it ruins the reputation."

"Gone With the Wind?"

"One of my favorites," said Ricky Dean, occupying the bar stool next to Heath's. "How you holding up?"

"Pissed. And sad."

"I hear ya."

"You probably have to deal with this all the time."

"Yep. Almost every damn day."

"So what do we do now?"

"Same thing I always say at every car wreck. 'Move on, nothing to see here.'"

"Ain't that a bitch?"

"Yep." Ricky Dean motioned to the bartender for a beer.

"Hey, I'm sorry for being such a hothead. I know it's not your fault. Or Potter's."

"No harm done Mr. Reporter Man. You gave it the ol' college try. Sometimes shit just don't come together."

Heath took another sip of his suds. “You know, it was my dream guy who directed me to that auction, to that box.”

Ricky Dean shook his head and laughed. “And how well did that work out?”

“Not as good as I'd hoped. Maybe instead of asking him who murdered Tilda Pollack, I should've asked him how to convict the murderer of Tilda Pollack.”

“Hindsight.”

“So what happens to Tilda's jewelry?”

“Well, I reckon we'll hold on to it for a while. That's what I told Franny. May wait to see what Briggs has to say when he takes office in January. I don't see him pursuing this case. He's a far bigger wimp than Jake Potter ever was.”

“And then? Will it be given back to Franny?”

“Maybe. Would you like to deliver it?”

Heath paused, then said, “You know, actually, I would. She deserves as much.”

“I could probably arrange that.”

Life went on as much as it always seemed to do before. Heath covered his beat. Bridget Parker covered hers. Trace Philips, the Republic's young reporter, did his thing.

Still, the gall of knowing Fox Ragsworth murdered that girl ate at Heath. He was angry not only at that, but that his dream had led to this. There had been no resolution, no justice. He felt betrayed.

Impertinent as it was, Heath wanted to see Fox Ragsworth for himself, to look the old man in the eyes. To look into the eyes of a rapist and murderer.

On a Thursday after work, he drove to the rest home where Fox Ragsworth was kept, Applewood Acres. He carried with him a small vase of flowers with card attached. Removing his reporter's ID beforehand, he entered the facility.

“I have a delivery for a... Mr. Ragsworth?” he told the receptionist, a young lady with more interest in her smartphone than the visitor.

“That's fine. Just leave it here, and we'll take it to his room. Thank you.”

“No, I was told to deliver it in person.”

“Who are you with?”

“Happy's Flower Shop.”

“Happy's Flower Shop? Never heard of 'em.”

“It's just off Route 45.”

The receptionist popped her bubblegum. “OK. He's in room 9B. Down that way, to the left. And keep it quiet. Strict orders. Set it on the table inside and walk out.”

“Gotcha,” Heath replied, with a wink.

As he made his way down the hall, he congratulated himself on being such a good bullshitter. First, there was no Happy's Flower Shop. Second, there was no Route 45. A quick internet search on her part would've put an end to his clandestine visit quickly.

The door to room 9B was shut. Slowly, Heath turned the handle. The room was almost completely dark. A small lamp on the table in the room its only source of illumination. He set down the vase. He heard the labored breathing of a form on a bed. Moving closer, he saw the old man, bald, extremely thin, seemingly asleep.

Something compelled him to do what he did next. It was something he would not have normally done, but the weight of knowledge he'd learned, the injustice of the situation, prompted him to speak.

“I know you did it,” he said, not loudly, with little emotion. “You killed that girl.”

The man continued to sleep.

"You may think you got away with it," Heath continued. "But I know it. Others now know it. God knows it. I hope you'll burn in hell for what you did to that girl."

With that, the man in the bed slowly opened his eyes. He didn't move his head, but his breathing changed.

Heath leaned in. With what little light there was in the room, he looked into the man's eyes. They were dark, but cognizant.

"Yes, you heard me. You heard what I said."

The old man shuddered, and exhibited a moan. His hands trembled as they lay powerless beside him, unable to rise, unable to defend him from the truth.

It was enough, Heath thought. He picked up the vase, turned and exited the room.

That same night, in his dreams, Heath again entered the white room.

"Why?" he asked the old man with white hair, still fiddling with his papers.

"Is that a question?" replied the man, insinuating a better question should be asked.

Heath wasn't sure how to answer the man who now questioned him.

“You asked. I told. You now know,” the old man said, unprompted.

“It's not fair,” he protested.

“No, it's not. There is much in life which isn't fair.”

Heath, aware at this point he was obviously losing the debate, had nothing to say. He'd not prepared any question to ask.

“Indianapolis.”

“What?”

“Bogan's Flower Shop.”

Heath knew, instantly. He was speaking of Anne, her home, her workplace. How the old man knew, he could not understand.

“Be very sure. A price will be paid.”

“Be sure of what?” Heath inquired. “What price?”

“You only get one more after this.”

“One more? One more what?”

As in the last dream, the specter pointed towards an object behind Heath, to his right. Again, as Heath turned to look, he was pulled from the room with great force, to awaken as before.

"Heath, come 'ere."

He got up and entered Constance's office.

"Close the door."

"Hell, what did I do now?" he asked, flippantly. He knew from the look on Constance's face, however, that something grave had happened.

"Were you at Applewood Acres last Thursday?"

Busted. And he wasn't going to lie to his boss, also his friend.

"Yes."

Constance sighed. "We've got trouble."

"Yeah?"

"I just got a phone call from Valerie Ragsworth. She's mad as a hornet. Before that, her idiot son Ernie called me."

"Screw her, screw them both," Heath replied, without hesitation.

"Yeah, well guess what Sherlock Holmes, she said if I don't fire you, she will drop all their advertising with us. All of it. And convince her business partners to do the same."

"The hell?"

Constance leaned back in her chair, and tapped on her desk with a pen. "She also said she's considering pressing charges against you for harassment and trespassing. And suing the paper for libel if we in any way mention the family – Fox, her, Ernie – in regards to the Pollack case. They caught you on security camera."

"Huh?"

"From what I've been told, they have you entering Applewood Acres. They have you talking to the receptionist. They have you walking down the hall. They have you entering Fox Ragsworth's room. Now, don't give me any bullshit, what were you doing there?"

"I wanted to see him. I wanted to see the face of the son of a bitch."

"And that's all? We have numerous photos of him in our files."

"No, I knew what he looked like. What he looked like then. I wanted to look into his eyes. I wanted to see the bastard himself. As he is now."

"Well guess what, Heath. The bastard was pronounced dead this morning. Bridget's working on his obituary now. It will be front page."

Heath took a seat. "Holy shit."

"Did you say something to him?"

"The truth?"

"Yes, the truth."

“I told him I knew what he did and others knew, and he was going to burn in hell.”

Constance looked away and shook her head.

“Yeah, holy shit for sure. Dammit, you've put us in a bad position.”

“I... put us... in a bad position?” Heath asked, incredulously. “For telling the truth? For trying to get justice for that girl? For telling him what I thought of him?”

“Heath, this paper can't run without that old witch. God's honest truth. Sixty percent of our advertising. She owns the plant, the bank, half the real estate in town. She would drop loans to businesses advertising with us, pull the leases of others.”

Heath knew it was true. Constance wouldn't lie about that.

“So... if I fire you, Valerie said she will forget the whole thing happened, will not press any charges, and life goes on here as before. No harm done. They can't prove you did anything to kill the old buzzard. He's been on his deathbed for years, but they sure as hell can make things damn difficult for you, for us.”

Heath said nothing.

Again, Constance spoke.

“Heath, I'm not going to fire you. Valerie Ragsworth can go screw herself. I have never let go of a good reporter because of an advertiser being bitchy, and I never will.”

The realization of what was at stake hit home. Within seconds, Heath knew what he had to do.

“No. You're right. You are not going to fire me – I quit.”

CHAPTER 8

What choice did he have? Losing that much advertising, all at once, the *Brighton Falls Republic* would be finished. It wasn't just his livelihood at stake. He, Constance, Bridget, Trace, all the salespeople, the paper delivery people – all would be without a job, and there would be no local daily paper. All because he pursued this case. Truth, in this instance, was indeed costly.

It was the first time he'd ever seen Constance shed tears. No one else knew, yet. He waited until everyone else had gone home for the day before clearing out the belongings in his desk. She would inform them in the morning of his departure. And she would tell Valerie Ragsworth that Heath Hawkins was no longer an employee at the paper.

He thought about the dream. Now unemployed, he pondered driving to Indianapolis, which was close to his hometown of Brewster. There was indeed a Bogan's Flower Shop there. Heath had put his researching skills to work. Anne was listed as still living in the area. And she did have a social media account, though her profile picture was blurry and small. Details about her life, though, remained sparse.

The dream man's warning, however, remained haunting.

“Be very sure. A price will be paid.”

What was that supposed to mean? Would acting upon this knowledge turn out like the Booth papers, or like the Tilda Pollack case?

And his crush on Anne Ross as a teen? It seemed preposterous to just show up in Indianapolis and say “Hey Anne, how are you? I'm Heath Hawkins. Remember me? I worshiped the ground you walked on. Want to go out for a drink?” No, he would plan a better way to connect. He had to think this through. There were many things to be considered.

Besides, he had unfinished business in Brighton Falls. Fox Ragsworth's funeral service was tomorrow.

That morning he put on his best suit and tie. Now jobless, and soon homeless unless he found some work, Heath attempted to eke out one small bit of satisfaction for himself. Though Fox Ragsworth had died four days after his visit to Applewood Acres, and it was surely a coincidence, Heath wondered if the conversation is what finally pushed the old man over the cliff. But did that make him, Heath, a murderer? No, he told himself. Words themselves don't kill. But if truth does, so be it.

He stopped by a flower shop, bought a dozen red roses, and took off for the cemetery.

Brighton Falls Memorial Cemetery held graves dating back to the mid-1700s, though the elements had reduced most of those old, limestone grave markers to incoherent lumps. Heath had spent many a time walking the grounds. It was serene and secluded. A good place to take in some nature and art. To clear the mind.

Fox Ragsworth's funeral was scheduled for 11 a.m. It was a private service, with only select mourners present. As Heath drove his car onto the grounds, he saw a sheriff's cruiser parked near the entrance, having escorted the funeral party to the cemetery. He pulled alongside and parked, then exited the car.

"Well don't you look spiffy, Officer Irish McMurphy?"

"Heath, what the hell you doing here?" asked Ricky Dean, who was wearing his official sheriff's deputy uniform.

"I'm here to pay my respects."

Ricky Dean had a concerned, surprised, even suspicious, look on his face. "Heath, you go anywhere within 100 yards of the service, I will kick you out of here. Private ceremony."

"I know that."

"You know? Then why are you here?"

"Like I said, I'm here to pay my respects."

Ricky Dean now looked puzzled. "I'm serious. You WILL be arrested for interrupting the service. I'm begging you, please, don't do it."

"I'm not interrupting anything," he replied. "I'm going over there." He pointed to a different part of the cemetery from where Ragsworth was being laid to rest.

With that, he walked away, Ricky Dean watching him every step. The detective couldn't help but admire his friend. It took some guts for him to be at this cemetery, on this day.

At the exact same time Fox Ragsworth's crippled, emaciated remains were being interred under an ornate granite memorial, Heath placed a dozen roses on the small, simple grave marker of Matilda Marie Pollack.

Bigger paper, better money, good benefits, a faster paced news cycle. Heath was thriving professionally at the *Indianapolis Daily Press*. It was a significant adjustment from the lazy local he'd left a year before, to be sure. He dabbled in a little of everything, but most of his assignments were on businesses.

He still kept in touch with those he'd left behind in Brighton Falls: Ricky Dean, Constance, even Bridget, who had received her shot at covering the crime beat and actually performed satisfactorily. No misspellings of Judge John Paul Jones. It was a good start.

As expected, Bart Briggs ran unopposed and won the prosecutor's seat. And, like Potter, he had no intention of continuing the investigation into Tilda Pollack's death. Ricky Dean told Heath he had approached the new prosecutor with the evidence – Briggs barely looked at it. "We're not wasting taxpayer money investigating a dead man." Back into storage went the jewelry, the jewelry box, the note and the case files, for the time being.

Late in the year, the lawsuit against Ragsworth Industries was settled out of court. Valerie Ragsworth agreed to pay for most of the medical costs and offered some severance, but the larger issue of worker safety was left unresolved. By every measure, she'd won, and the former, and current, employees had lost.

Hearing the news galled him, but Fox Ragsworth's pristine postmortem reputation still nagged him more.

“Something bothering you?”

“Naw, nothing.”

“You've had this pissed look on your face all day. Did they cancel your membership in the Jaded Fellowship of Cynical Reporters?”

Theo Woods, was the *Daily Press's* lead crime reporter. Outgoing, handsome, quick-witted, the two had become fast friends after Heath had been hired on following his time at the *Republic*.

“Is it about that lawsuit?”

“Not just that. The whole situation.”

“Oh, that girl.” Theo was quite familiar with the story.

"Yeah. I feel like... I feel like I didn't do all I should've done, you know?"

Theo shook his head and gave a half laugh, followed by faux sympathy. "Oh, I'm sorry, I didn't realize reporters were superheros. Nice cape you got there."

Though Theo was only a few years younger than Heath, he was far more energetic. Too, Heath often wondered if Theo had years' more wisdom stored up under that jet black hair of his.

"You're right."

"Of course I am." Theo didn't lack for chutzpah. "Let's close this down and go grab a drink."

Heath shut down his laptop, grabbed his bag and camera and the two headed for the elevator.

"You said she threatened to shut down your old paper, pull the advertising, right?"

"Yep. The old crone hit us right in the money bags."

"Are you employed there now?"

Heath stopped and looked at him. No, no he wasn't.

"If you aren't employed there, and haven't been for some time, what threat does she pose to the paper now?"

He hadn't thought of that. Heath realized he'd been far too wrapped up in the case, the move back to Indiana, and his own thoughts.

"None I guess. I was the target of her wrath. She used threats against the paper as a club against me."

"And if what you write is factual, can she legitimately sue you for libel?"

"No, not really I reckon."

"So quit being a pussy. Tell your story already. Send it to whoever you think will run it. Send it anonymously. Or put your name on it. Doesn't matter. If the case isn't reopened, big deal, what have you lost? Nothing. If the story smears the dead, dirty pedophile rapist and makes his old lady cry and his fat, stupid kid piss himself, good. Get the damn thing off your chest, and out of your head already."

Heath nodded. Theo was right. Absolutely correct.

"Let's go get that drink, Batman," said the younger, and probably wiser, reporter.

After he drank, he wrote. That very night. First draft, second draft, rinse, repeat, third draft.

Heath's story revisited the circumstances of Tilda's rape and murder as well as the incomplete investigation which had followed. It told of the discovery of her belongings and the note in the jewelry box, although he left out "how" he'd known where to find them. It traced the provenance of the jewelry box to the family, and tied the handwritten note to the family patriarch. It showcased the indifference of the two prosecutors and the threats to the paper by the family matriarch and her son.

The retelling was matter of fact. One might have called it cold, obtuse. However, Heath did provide one sop to emotion at the end.

> *"Though no one will never appear in a court of law to answer for the crimes committed against Tilda, her death should not be callously brushed aside. Matilda 'Tilda' Marie Pollack was a real girl, whose body lies in a real grave, and whose mother still cries real tears. Though the perpetrator of the crime skirted justice through the affluence of his family and by his own passing, his name should be remembered in ignominy as much as his victim's name is remembered in sad fondness."*

Nowhere within the story, not in any instance, did Heath use the names "Fox Ragsworth," "Valerie Ragsworth," or "Ernie Ragsworth."

Upon reviewing it, Theo at first thought not fingering the the culprits by name was a cop-out, but once he learned just how small Brighton Falls was, and how everyone reading the story there would know exactly who the "patriarch," "matriarch," and "son" were, he found it brilliant.

Heath had retained digital photos of much of the evidence, including the note, earrings, ring and watch. He also had a copy of Tilda's high school portrait, taken months before her demise. These would illustrate the tale, putting a human face to her ghost.

"This is not going away. Not even close." His own words echoed back to him.

Heath sent copies of the story not only to Constance, but to all the nearby local papers, and even to some of the bigger papers in the area. He hoped a few national publications would pick it up. It was offered for free. He sought no money. He submitted it, giving the publishers the choice to run it anonymously, or not. He was submitting the article as a freelancer, not on behalf of the *Daily*

Press, the *Republic*, or any other news outlet. The Ragsworths might be furious, but they couldn't touch him.

What did he hope to see happen? That was the question. Even he wasn't entirely sure. He settled on the satisfying notion that perhaps a few people would remember Fox Ragsworth as a rapist and a murderer who escaped the noose versus the picture of him as an innocuous, handsome, business magnate who spent his last years quietly mouldering in pastoral Applewood Acres.

Theo did advise Heath that while unlikely, he indeed could be sued. “People file lawsuits for everything, anything, and nothing,” he warned.

“What'll they get? The $640 in my savings account? My $12,000 retirement? My 13-year-old Nissan?”

“Maybe she'll send her tub o' lard son to kick your ass.”

“That would presume he's sober enough to drive.”

“No way, no way in hell,” Constance told Heath over the phone after receiving a copy of his story.

Heath didn't expect Constance to run it. A year removed, she still felt the Ragsworth ax over the paper's head. “But this will run in the other papers,” she said. “It's good. Great even.”

“Thanks chief.”

“You doing OK?”

“Yeah, not bad.”

“We miss you here.” Hearing that meant more to Heath than praise for anything he'd written.

CHAPTER 9

The story did run. First, in the nearby dailies and weeklies. Then the *Atlantic* picked it up. Heath couldn't help but be amused by a snippet in his author bio.

> *"In addition to his work as a reporter for the* Brighton Falls Republic *and the* Indianapolis Daily Press*, Hawkins also discovered the missing pages from the diary of John Wilkes Booth, which are now enshrined in the National Archives."*

In this regard, his earlier notoriety helped.

The reaction was largely positive. Like Theo had said, even if it didn't result in any legal action being initiated, there was a satisfaction in knowing the truth was out there. No more secrets. No more shadows. Heath received emails, and even a few letters, from people who expressed appreciation for his story.

Interestingly, there appeared to be no repercussions from the Ragsworths. Had they finally been humbled? Or perhaps they were unaware? Heath found the lack of reaction from the Ragsworth camp, the silence, unsettling.

It had been more than a year since he'd shared a conversation with his dream friend. Heath had not intentionally sought to wander back to the white room, but he did find it somewhat curious the dreams had not returned.

"Be very sure. A price will be paid," the man said. "You only get one more after this." Those words, the image, remained lucid. The meaning? Not so much.

It was a chance encounter with a former classmate that once again brought thoughts of Anne Ross to the fore. Heath took a quick trip to his hometown, Brewster, a suburb of Indianapolis. Much of it remained unchanged over the years, not yet being the victim of urban, or suburban, sprawl.

He visited the gravesite of his parents. They'd died young. Far too young. Mom, of cancer. Dad, in a car wreck. He laid daisies on the grave, his mother's favorite.

He drove past the new school. "Home of the Brewster Bobcats!" proclaimed the flashing LED sign installed out front. Though he felt somewhat sad the old school had been demolished, he was happy for today's students. Climate control that worked, textbooks on touchpads, comfortable learning spaces, a less-restricted dress code – things only dreamed of during his student days.

Before heading home, he stopped by Duffy's Diner. It used to be Dicky's Diner, but the new owner wasn't too keen on the old name.

"Oh my God!" a familiar voice exclaimed upon his entry.

"Hey there," said Heath. An apron-clad, flaming haired Clara Clyde ran up and gave him a hug.

"It's been so long! It's been years!" she said, finally letting go of him.

"No doubt."

"Where have you been? What have you been doing?" Heath actually took pleasure in the fact not everyone had kept abreast of his journalistic endeavors.

“Just doing the reporter thing.”

“That's SO cool!” she gushed.

“It can be.”

“Oh my God, it's been so long. What brings you back to town?”

“Just passing through. Stopped by to pay my respects, see how things look here nowadays.”

Clara laughed, “Nothing changes here in Brewster. You know that. Not much anyway.”

“No, I reckon not.”

“Your voice sounds a little different.” Heath hadn't really noticed, but yes, yes it had.

“Eleven years in Virginia will do that,” he replied.

“Southern boy now.”

“Yep!”

Though Clara should have been waiting tables, although it wasn't busy, she sat down with Heath and talked and talked and talked: Her first marriage. Her second marriage. Her five children. Her job. Heath didn't mind. It was nice to catch up. Clara had been a potential girlfriend in school. It had never become serious. But then, really, what relationships in high school become or stay serious?

“So you're living in Indy?”

“Yep, about two miles from the paper. There's some days I'd walk, but I need to have my car handy for assignments.”

“Have you met the president? Have you met any celebrities?”

It was Heath's turn to laugh. “No, not really. I did get to shake hands with Bonnie Franklin once. That was cool.”

“Bonnie Franklin?”

“You know, redhead, actress, 'One Day at a Time?'”

“Ahhh...” Clara said, although he was not sure she really knew who Bonnie Franklin was. “Well you didn't have a thing for redheads anyway. There was a brunette you were hot for, though.”

“Oh yeah?”

“Remember Anne Ross? She was in here yesterday.”

Hearing that name pulled the breath from Heath's lungs. “Oh, really?” he replied, suddenly dry-throated.

“Yes. Don't you remember?”

“Remember...?”

"Oh my God, Heath! You were so in love with her."

Heath was embarrassed, but offered a smile. "She was nice."

"Nice? Heath, you followed her around like a lost puppy dog. Everyone could tell. Even she knew."

Now Clara had his undivided attention. "Everyone? Even her?" he asked.

"Yes, you big goof."

"And she was here yesterday?"

"Uh huh. Sat right here where we are. We talked."

"About?"

"Everything: Families. Brewster. High school. The food here. Guys."

Heath ran his left index finger along the rim of his coffee cup. "So did she, I mean, uh, did she say anything about me?"

"As a matter of fact, she did."

"What was it?"

"Hmmm... let me think. We were talking about the old days, back in school. And I said she still looked so pretty, just as pretty as she did then. Of course, she was all like, 'Stop it.' And I said, 'No, you really do.' And she said something about being an old ugly duckling or something."

"Really? She was beautiful."

"I know, right? So anyway, that's what I said. And I told her there was a guy in high school who just thought she was the most beautiful thing ever. Remember you kept asking me for information on her, even though she and I weren't best friends or anything. Just good friends."

Clara was right. Heath did recall recruiting her to spy on Anne. Kind of a dick move, really, he thought in retrospect.

"Wow, and so you told her I thought that?"

"Uh huh. And you know what she told me?"

"Yes?"

Clara giggled, "She told me, 'Oh Heath Hawkins. He was such a cutie. Good looking, smart. I really liked him. So quiet, though.'"

"Shut up! She did NOT say that!"

A look of indignation took hold of Clara's face. "She most certainly did!"

Heath appeared dubious. "So she said she liked me? Me?"

"Yes, and we both agreed you were cute...and quiet. Too quiet."

"Huh. Go figure. So then what?"

"Not too much else. Other stuff."

"So... where is she living now?"

"Indy. Like you."

"Is she dating anyone?"

"No, I don't think so. She was married, briefly. Ended in divorce. Guess the guy was a real tool. No kids, or none she mentioned. It's a shame you weren't here yesterday. Could have been fun."

Heath left Clara a generous tip. Not rentworthy, but a $20 tip for a $7.50 lunch is nothing at which one should scoff. She gave him another hug, and a kiss on the cheek, upon his departure.

In return, however, Clara had given him a tip which was much more than generous. She'd given him confirmation. Or at least what he viewed as confirmation. Was it really true? Did Anne really like him back then? He wasn't sure she'd even noticed him, much less liked him. There can be, of course, a huge chasm between "Like" and "Love." Heath wondered if the gap was surmountable.

Again, the dream. The white-haired man knew the question that had been on his mind. And the mystery of Anne Ross was one that had long tormented him. Why had he been so standoffish? Why so timid? Granted, he never liked the spotlight, but Anne was not a spotlight. There was something about her he found extremely intimidating. As if he would trip and fall on his face if he dared enter her proximity.

To Heath, it had always been more than a school-age crush. A magnetic quality about Anne drew him in. Yet his own insecurities, his self doubt, had pushed him away. The truth was, he never felt worthy, about her, about much of anything.

So here he was, filled with hope. She truly had been the only one for him, he thought, a silly thought given they had barely interacted. Single, still beautiful (according to Clara), and near. How to do this, he wondered?

"Hey Mr. Reporter Man, you sitting down?" said a familiar voice when Heath answered his phone.

"Ricky Dean! How are you? And yes, I'm sitting down."

"This'll eat your cornbread. Yesterday, investigators from the Virginia Attorney General's office came into the station. Missing Children's Division," he disclosed.

"What?"

"Yessireeebob. They wanted to see the Tilda Pollack files."

"Holy shit, you're joking."

"Nope. Now I'm not making any promises here, but they spent a good five hours looking through it. They made photocopies, took pictures. They had me fill out a statement, asked me some questions."

Heath listened, stunned.

"Now I'm not expecting them to do anything about Fox, obviously, but maybe take a closer looksee into other victims, missing kids. Maybe Tilda wasn't the only one."

"So what do you think? Is this serious? What does this mean?"

"Don't know. But I'd say someone must have brought your story to their attention. In Virginia, the law don't get no bigger than the Attorney General, except for the FBI, of course."

"Wow," Heath said, genuinely shocked.

"Now, don't be surprised if you get a call from them, to ask you some questions. Who knows, maybe you'll get to testify."

"I will. I damn sure will. Did they question anyone else?"

"They talked to the sheriff. And Briggs. Not sure what he told 'em. I wasn't in the room for that conversation, but he sure didn't look happy walking out."

CHAPTER 10

Heath was feeling as good as he'd ever felt. Or as good as he ever remembered feeling. Tilda's murderer might be dead, but a chance at having a final, definitive answer – the truth, out in the open – would be better than nothing, and that day seemed to be approaching. And there was Anne. He felt the time was right to make something happen.

He requested Friday off from work. The entire week leading up to that, Heath went on a crash-course diet. The middle-aged-man diet. He wanted to shed a few pounds. The belly must shrink. And the hair? Well, he didn't want things to get too crazy – no hair coloring – but he got it trimmed. His dream girl would just have to live with his gray temples and the thinning on top. He was approaching 40, he told himself. There's only so much one can cover up that won't eventually be revealed.

And what to wear? Should he pick up a new outfit? And how would he approach her? Should he walk into the garden center as if to purchase something, then casually act surprised that she was there? Should he just walk straight up to her, profess his love, pick her up in his arms and carry her out the door? Heath decided to proceed with a method in between the two. He would go in, under the pretense of a purchase, then strike up a conversation.

Again and again, Heath practiced his potential dialog."

"Hey, you look familiar. Do I know you?"

"Why hello, Anne. Fancy meeting you here."

"This is funny, but you look like someone I know."

"Anne, it's been a long time, but I thought there's something I should tell you."

"Hey, do you have change for a $50?"

"I like peonies. How about you?"

"What potting soil do you recommend?"

"Garden gnomes. Why would anyone want a garden gnome?"

"Anne, I think you're the most beautiful woman in the world."

No matter what pickup line Heath used in his monologue, each and every one sounded utterly foolish. Plan B: Walk in, look around, let happen what is going to happen, he decided.

Friday came. Heath turned off his phone and computer. No distractions. No chatter. He needed to concentrate on the task at hand.

He did his typical morning routine. Coffee, breakfast – two pieces of toast, lightly buttered – shower, teeth brushing, get dressed. It would be warm out today, August 25. The summer humidity of Indiana matched, if not exceeded, the humidity of Virginia, he felt. He would dress comfortably, but not too comfortably: a light blue pullover collared shirt, brand new jean shorts. A very light dab of cologne on his neck.

Looking in the mirror, he was perturbed to detect a pimple on his forehead. "God almighty," he said. "Seriously?" Acting the part of a lovesick teenager, despite his age, has that effect, he thought. The zit was popped and its remnant hopefully would be overlooked.

He didn't want to show up when the shop was too busy. He wanted a chance to speak with her without too much chance of interruption. Three o' clock should work, he reckoned. Bogan's was open from 8 a.m. until 7 p.m. The early hours would likely be crowded with the up-and-at-em gardeners. The late hours would be packed with the afterwork crowd getting their gardening supplies for the weekend ahead. Three would be best, definitely, yes. He just hoped she hadn't called off work. Prayed, actually.

Lunch was skipped. His stomach was too nervous, and he didn't want to be burping his pickup line when the time came.

Bogan's Garden Center sat in a strip mall, of sorts. Access to traffic had been closed at both ends of the plaza where the shop was located, and repaved into a walking, biking, skateboarding area. The rear of Bogan's, however, had loading docks where the "people of the soil" could load supplies directly into their pickup trucks.

Heath parked his car and got out. The August sun was oppressive, and he started sweating the moment he left the vehicle's air conditioned comfort. He walked to the plaza and searched for a shady spot. Mostly mothers with children roamed the grounds. A few old timers, too. It was only 2:50 p.m. He had vowed to himself he would wait until

3. What's 10 minutes in comparison to more than 20 years? Patience.

At 2:50 p.m., 600-some miles away, Becky, the handicapped woman in the wheelchair, became agitated, rolling her head from side to side.

"What is it, hon?" her caregiver asked.

"Traveler," she said. "Tra-vel-er."

"What's that? What're you talking about?"

"Hurt."

Heath sat on a bench under the shade of a tree, trying to stay cool. He watched as a few shoppers entered and exited the garden center. He tried to catch a glimpse inside, but the windows were tinted. He looked at his watch – 2:53. "Damn," he thought. "I should've waited later to come here. I'm a sweaty mess." He felt like he was going to pass out. He also felt it strange that he should be so nervous, a throwback to his younger days. Again with the past doubts. Why had he run off that stage after the spelling bee? Why had he not been bold and talked to Anne back then? Heck, why had he cowered from the spotlight at the university press conference? He had led the charge in finding

Tilda's murderer, and yet found himself falling back into his awkward, shy persona.

"No," he told himself. "Today, that changes. For good."

Nonetheless, he detected a sense of foreboding. He couldn't pinpoint it exactly, but there was something askew, not right.

The minutes seemed like hours. He looked at his watch again – 2:57. He then asked himself: "Why do I have to walk in there at 3? I'm not a slave to the clock. I'M the one who sets the time."

He rose with determination and walked towards the front entrance. The closer he got, the less dark the shop's windows appeared. He began to see images, shapes inside. At the checkout, was it... was it Anne?

Yes, it had to be. It was. There was no mistaking it. There she stood, smiling, wearing a dark green Bogan's Garden Center apron and a nametag. She was radiant. Not the same girl from high school – no one stays exactly the same – but she was beautiful, absolutely beautiful.

Heath felt something hit him, in the back. It felt like a hammer. Worse even. Then another hammer blow to the back. Stunned by the sudden pain, he looked down. His light blue shirt was turning dark.

He heard a woman's scream, detected a scramble behind him, rushed footsteps, voices, angry voices.

The sun hurt his eyes as he tried to right himself. More screaming. The darkness on his shirt now hit the sidewalk. His ears rung and felt flooded with waves of water. Now on his hands, he looked up and saw Anne. Anne! She had come out of the shop and was looking at him, her head tilted, a look of curiosity on her face. Then, an expression of great concern.

Heath felt hands on him. The hands rolled him onto his side. Then he felt himself lifted by the hands, facing him up to the blinding sun in the sky. Then darkness.

CHAPTER 11

The darkness lasted for a time. Heath looked around. He felt without bearing, lost. The pain he'd felt still lingered, but had started to fade.

He was walking, but to where, he was not sure. His mind began talking to him. Was he dead? What had happened? Why had everything disappeared? After stumbling around in almost total darkness for a span of time undetermined, he detected a sliver of light. He moved towards it. As he closed in on it, he saw it was a partially open door. He wondered if he should open it, then decided what was behind the door was likely no worse than wandering fruitlessly in the dark.

His dream. The white room. The white-haired, tan-faced man was there. But was he dreaming or dead?

"Your job now is to live," said the strange figure, still shuffling his mysterious papers.

"To live?"

"Yes."

"What happened to me? I was walking... to see Anne... and..."

"It is of no concern at this moment. You will learn the details later."

"Anne... is she...?"

"She is well. You job now is to live. You need to recover. And you will."

Heath stood silent for a bit. He remembered the words of the white-haired man from his prior dream.

"You said I had one more. One more what?"

"You will have an opportunity, in the future, to ask one more question."

At least the man was more forthcoming with information during this visit, Heath mused.

The man gave Heath a smile, a look which gave him the impression his dream friend could read his very thoughts. Then the man pointed, as in past dreams. Heath cringed, awaiting the sensation of being violently pulled from the room as before.

“Look,” the man said, still pointing.

Heath turned to where the man was directing. On the wall was a mirror.

“Look,” the white-haired man urged.

He moved closer to the mirror. It had a dark, old appearance, like one which had sat in an abandoned home, its silver flaking and fading, the glass cloudy. As he got closer, however, it became clearer, a mist suddenly lifting.

Stepping up to the mirror, he opened his eyes, fully, completely, without fear. In the mirror he saw a blonde-haired boy. Perplexed, he squinted his eyes. He was looking at his own reflection.

“But... how?” he asked.

“That is who you are. Who you really are. Your soul. You have the soul of a traveler.”

He kept looking at the boy in the mirror. Almost a teen, really.

“A few years ago, you would have seen a boy much younger. With tears in his eyes. Hiding.”

Heath couldn't speak. A speechlessness overtook him.

"Some never seek the truth, some never grow, never mature," said his spectral benefactor, walking closer to join him at the mirror. "They choose not to see. They are as old and wretched here as they are in life. They live outside that door, in that darkness. A choice they've made. No interest in the truth."

As he stared at his past self, or, his current, true soul, Heath saw the image of the white-haired man join his younger self in the mirror.

"Now," he said, "Look in this mirror."

Heath hadn't noticed the second mirror, mounted near the first. He stepped to that mirror, and saw himself, as he was, now. Older, gray at the temples.

"This is your earthly reality," the white-haired man told him.

Behind his current self, sharing this mirror, was a mangled, palsied, crippled woman in a wheelchair. Heath recognized her, though it took a moment to remember her name.

"Becky?"

"It is time. Go back. Your job now is to live."

“Heath? Heath? Can you hear me?”

“Yes,” he said. Or thought he said. His ears heard and he wanted to speak but his mouth was not cooperating.

“Heath, my name is Stella. I'm your nurse today. Heath, can you hear me?”

“Y... yes.”

“Heath, I'm going to raise your bed a little, OK?”

Heath nodded. Or thought he did. He heard the whirr of the bed's electric motor raise the head of the hospital bed, bringing the top half of him more upright.

“Heath, can you open your eyes?”

“Yes.”

“Heath, open your eyes for me.”

“Yes.”

He heard a giggle, which must be this Stella person.

“Open your eyes, Heath.”

“Oh,” he thought. “She wants me to open my eyes.” He did, slowly. The world looked funny to him. He wanted to close his eyes again.

“How are you feeling today?”

He wasn't sure how to answer that question. What exactly was this so-called “today?” And how did he feel?

“OK,” he answered. More a guess. He wasn't certain on this point.

“Heath, what's your last name?”

“Hawkins.”

“Good Heath. What's your birthday?”

“September 7.”

“What type of car do you drive?”

“Nissan.” Although he remembered he hoped to upgrade soon.

Heath ventured to open his eyes again. He did, closed them, then opened them again.

“What day is it?” he asked.

“Saturday.”

“Saturday?”

“Uh huh.” He felt Stella, or someone, messing with his hands and his arms.

“Are you thirsty Heath?”

Yes, he was thirsty. Quite thirsty.

“Heath, would you like some ice chips?”

He nodded. Stella shook her head, signifying to him he would be fine. Coming out of his anesthesia, he was now responding to questions after being asked two or three times in contrast to five or six. The earlier Q-and-A sessions had slipped from his memory.

He then felt the most wonderful thing in the world hit his lips. A cool spoonful of small, chunky ice. It seemed to him he hadn't had a drink all his life up to that point.

“Heath, the doctor will be in shortly.”

“Hey... Stella?”

“Yes?”

“What day is it?”

The hammer he'd felt had been a bullet. Two actually. 158-grain lead round nose bullets to be precise. Shot from a Smith and Wesson Model 438 revolver.

“If he'd hit you with hollow points, youda been a goner,” said Ricky Dean.

“You don't say.” Heath was still in his bed at the hospital, and remained rather woozy coming out of surgery.

“Still he messed you up pretty good.”

"You know you're gonna have to repeat all this to me again, right?"

His cop buddy laughed. "I shoulda brought Nan with me. She's used to repeating herself after talking to me."

"So the doctor says I'm going to be OK, but I need to take it easy for a while."

"You're lucky, Mr. Reporter Man." Though still fuzzy on the finer details, Heath agreed.

"So what happens with Ernie?"

"They bury him. Or cremate him. Not sure yet."

"Huh?"

"He hung himself the night he shot you. Same night. They shoulda taken his belt before leaving him alone in the holding cell. Or not."

"So why'd he shoot me?"

"After that story ran, and got picked up, Valerie was pissed. Pissed her family had been implicated, but probably more angry there wasn't a damn thing she could do about it. She and big dummy had a blowup over it. Words were exchanged, accusations made. I guess she told him he was fired and was gonna kick him out. Reckon he felt he had nothing to lose, so he then drove here and tracked you down to make you pay for ruining his life."

"Huh? How did I do that?"

"Things still kinda sketchy, but it sounds like he blamed you. For ruining his reputation."

"Other than him being Fox's son, and a fat slob, how did I ruin HIS reputation?"

"When they brought him in, after the shooting, he was crying like a baby. A lot of 'em do. But he was very talkative. He didn't request an attorney. He just started blabbing. Confessed to the shooting, the reasons why, all that. There was more to it than Tilda. Things had been going on a long time."

"Things? Like?"

"Tilda Pollack may have been the only person Fox Ragsworth murdered, but she wasn't the only person he sexually abused. It sure as hell sounds like there were others. Including Ernie."

"Dear God."

He appreciated, more than he could express, Ricky Dean coming all the way from Virginia to see him.

Although his friend would have done it merely to check on him, he was also there on police business. Notified of the shooting, he'd caught a quick flight to Indy to question Ernie, and give the local law enforcement details on him. By the time he'd arrived, Ernie was cold and blue.

Assured Heath would be OK, Ricky bid him farewell and caught a flight back to The Old Dominion State.

Not long after he departed, Heath received another visitor.

"Hi."

"Anne... Hi."

"How are you feeling?"

"I think I'm doing OK." If my heart doesn't stop beating so hard, he thought to himself.

"That was something, wasn't it?"

"Sure was. Are you OK?" Heath asked.

"Oh I'm fine. I was a little shook up. It's not like you see someone get shot every day. Or someone you know get shot every day."

The realization that she was not only there, but admitted "knowing" him, made him feel like jumping out of the bed. Wooziness be damned!

Anne laid a vase filled with lilacs on his bedside table. "Thought these might cheer you up."

“They're beautiful. Get an employee discount?”

She gave him an odd look. “Yes, as a matter of fact. I work over at Bogan's Garden Center. How did you know?”

His cover was blown. “I know. You were the reason I was there.”

“Really?”

“Really.”

They talked for hours. She sat on the edge of his bed, both laughing, smiling, reminiscing. While he withheld the details of his dreams, he was open and honest about his feelings for her – then and now. He explained how, as a teen, he'd written her poems, drawn her portrait, composed countless letters professing his love, though none of his romantic offerings was ever delivered. He told her those feelings from his youth, however, had not subsided.

Partway through his confession, she'd taken his hand, holding it. As beautiful as he remembered her, he swore she was more beautiful now. Those eyes were even more deep and brown than he'd remembered.

“So that's my story,” he said. “Creeped out?”

“No, not at all. I think it's charming. I'm flattered. Incredibly flattered!”

"Thank you," he said.

"You're welcome, but why?"

"For coming to see me. For being here. For being you."

"Aww, you're so sweet. Why weren't you this sweet to me back then?"

"Because I was a coward."

"No."

"Yes. I had testicles, but no balls."

Anne laughed. "Teenage angst."

"Yep."

"I should probably get going. Can I come see you tomorrow?"

"Phhhhffttt... duh! If you don't come back I may perish and die. You not coming to see me tomorrow would be worse than getting shot."

"Stop. You're so dramatic." With that, she leaned over and kissed him on his forehead. Then, after a pause, looking into his eyes, her hands on his face, she kissed him gently on the lips. It was fortunate they'd removed his heart monitor. It might have exploded.

After a week in the hospital, and with the doctors relatively sure the bleeding had ceased, Heath was let go. Not only was it fortuitous he'd been shot with lead round nose bullets, which had passed through him relatively cleanly, the rounds had not caused any severe damage to his vital organs. The first had bypassed his left kidney, gone through his duodenum, and exited out his front. The second shot had gone between his left shoulder blade and clavicle, tearing up some ligaments, and also exiting. No one else had been hurt. Extremely dangerous, but not fatal.

His left arm in a sling, Theo picked him up. He was grateful to have a ride home, but wished it had been Anne.

Later he learned that Anne, once recovered from the initial shock of seeing bullets pass through his body, had rushed to him, pulled off her apron and tried to stop the bleeding. Did her quick response save his life? Probably.

Ernie had dropped the gun and taken off running, likely as shocked as everyone else in proximity was, but he didn't get far. The former athlete was tackled by two teens who had seen the whole thing happen, and they held him until the police arrived.

The irony of a former high school football hero being tackled didn't escape Heath. Nor did the irony of the fact that just as Franny Pollack had lost a daughter and a husband, Valerie Ragsworth too had lost a child and a spouse. Though they shared little else in life, they now shared pain, and grief.

Assured by his employer he still had a job, Heath spent the next two months recuperating. He saw Anne almost every day. She brought him meals, helped him with his household tasks. She also drove him to his followup appointments and physical therapy, as well as getting his mopey butt out of the apartment.

It was on one of these sojourns, to the local ice cream joint, that Anne related her own strange story.

"The night before you got shot, I had the weirdest dream."

"Tell me," he said.

"I was in a room. It was a strange room. Like everything was red. The floor, the walls, the door, everything in it."

"Hmmmm..."

"Anyway," Anne took another spoon of soft serve. "In this room was a girl. Or maybe a young lady, I think. She had a sad look on her face. I asked her why she was sad, but she wouldn't answer me."

"What did she look like?"

"She had this light brown hair. The funniest thing... it was poofy. You know, like 80s style."

Heath inhaled deeply, then let out a small sigh.

"You alright?" she asked.

"Yeah, I'm fine, go on."

"So, this girl, with the poofy hair. She was dressed in red too. She told me, 'Tomorrow, he comes.' And I was like, "Who?"

Heath listened, silently.

"Then she said, 'He knows the truth. He travels.' After that, I woke up."

A chill ran through Heath's body, and it wasn't the ice cream.

"It was quite vivid," Anne remarked.

CHAPTER 12

Heath met his spectral dream friend again soon after Anne had related her dream to him.

“You still may ask one more question,” the man in the white room informed Heath.

“No, I think I'll save it. That is, if I ever use it,” he answered. “I love her. She loves me. What more in life do I need to know?”

The dream man smiled and nodded.

Heath could have asked for anything: Where was the lost city of Atlantis? What killed the dinosaurs? What does God look like? What is the last digit of Pi? How many years to live did he have left? How many years did the world have left? He briefly pondered the mystery of how a dark-haired, handicapped woman on earth was in reality a white-haired, dream oracle man. Not to mention, why was he being given four questions, not three? Or a hundred?

No, Heath decided. His curiosity, his quest for truth, for the moment, was satisfied.

“Thank you... Becky,” Heath said, departing. The door shut behind him, quietly.

A year later, Heath returned to Brighton Falls. To see old friends, and to fulfill a task.

Anne came with him. She loved the drive, taking in the scenery from the Hoosier State through the Appalachians. To Heath, however, nothing seen on earth compared to her. It was all he could do to keep his eyes on the road.

They talked nonstop the entire trip. When they weren't talking, they sang along to every song that came on the radio.

He introduced her to Ricky Dean and his wife. Constance and his former coworkers. Some of the townspeople he'd grown to appreciate. And even Scotch, though this meeting happened only by chance as they strolled through the downtown.

Anne was enchanted with the old timer, who took off his ballcap, bowed courteously and kissed her hand.

“He's like this cute little hillbilly knight,” she gushed later. Heath rolled his eyes.

Becky, however, was nowhere to be found. “Perhaps on another trip back,” Heath decided.

Anne waited in the car as Heath knocked on the home's front door. In his hand was a gift box containing two earrings, a ring, and a wristwatch. The door was opened. She saw him hand the box to a woman who, lifting the box's lid, burst into tears. She fell to her knees in grief.

Anne momentarily considered getting out of the car, to offer the woman comfort, but then saw Heath help her to her feet. The weeping woman embraced him, and they said their goodbyes. The door was shut.

Tilda Pollack was home, at last.

As Heath and Anne traveled to Washington, D.C., to see the John Wilkes Booth papers on display at Ford's Theater, the pages of the diary he had discovered, she told him something she had not previously revealed.

“When you were laying there, after being shot, and I was trying to stop the bleeding...” Anne paused, overtaken with emotion as she briefly relived the moment.

Heath stayed silent as he drove, allowing her to collect herself.

“As you were laying there, you raised your right hand, and put your palm on my cheek. Your touch was so tender. Your eyes were open, and you were looking right at me, but it was like... you weren't really there. There was a calmness. You had a peace, a love in your eyes.”

“I don't remember that,” he confessed. “I wish I did.”

“It was at that moment I realized who you were. I said to myself, 'This looks like Heath Hawkins.' It was a funny thing to me, considering the condition you were in at that moment and how many years had passed. I wondered why you were here. You were there, on the ground, wounded, bleeding, and for all I knew you were dying, and I was thinking about how odd it was I recognized you. That's all I was thinking about at that moment. Isn't that strange?”

“No,” replied Heath. “I don't find it strange at all.”

POSTSCRIPT

“Hello, I'm Melissa Matthews. I called earlier? And you got the court order?”

“Yes, we did. Please have a seat. Let me grab her file.”

The attorney sat and waited while the clerk retrieved the requested records. A few moments later, the clerk returned, folder in hand.

“This is the one, right? Rebecca Cribbs?” asked the clerk.

“Yes, thank you.”

“Will you need photocopies when you're finished?”

"Please."

The clerk exited. The attorney opened the file folder and began reading.

> Child's name: Rebecca Matilda Cribbs
>
> Sex: Female
>
> Date of Birth: 09-10-1990
>
> Mother: Lydia Sue Cribbs
>
> Father: Ernest Richard Ragsworth
>
> Note: The child in question was born severely handicapped, with multiple medical ailments, but suffering primarily from cerebral palsy. While the listed father initially disputed paternity, both mother and father agreed to put the child up for adoption and signed documents relinquishing their parental rights accordingly. Child was delivered to the care of social services agents of the State of Virginia, 09-12-1990.

With photocopies made of this and other pertinent documents contained within the file, the attorney departed. Sitting in her car outside the courthouse, she placed a phone call.

"Hello?"

"Hey Glenda? It's me, Melissa."

"Hey."

"Just so you know, while Ernie disputed paternity, he did sign off on Becky's adoption. Between this and the DNA testing, I think it's rather straightforward. We've got an incredibly strong case here."

"Great news!"

"I know! Anyway, can you and Becky come over to the office tomorrow to sign some papers? Around 10?"

"Yes, I think we can do that. And thank you!"

"You bet. See you then. Bye."

"Bye."

The attorney smiled and shook her head. "Who would've thought it?" she said. "Now that Valerie Ragsworth is dead, Becky Cribbs, of all people, could become the sole heir to the Ragsworth estate."

ABOUT THE AUTHOR

Like the protagonist in "Four Questions," E. Scott Martin has worked as a small-town newspaper reporter, among other writing gigs. He enjoys creative writing, reading historical and biographical works, eating delicious grilled foods, and participating in trivia contests. He spends an inordinate amount of time trimming his mustache.

32291516R10083

Made in the USA
Columbia, SC
05 November 2018